PULP

PULP, July 2020.
First printing. Published by Image Comics, Inc. Office of publication: 2701 NW Vaughn St., Suite 780, Portland,
OR 97210. Copyright © 2020 Basement Gang, Inc. All rights reserved. "PULP," its logos, and the likenesses of all
characters herein are trademarks of Basement Gang, Inc., unless otherwise noted. "Image" and the Image Comics
logos are registered trademarks of Image Comics, Inc. No part of this publication may be reproduced or transmitted,
in any form or by any means (except for short excerpts for journalistic or review purposes), without the express
written permission of Basement Gang, Inc., or Image Comics, Inc. All names, characters, events, and locales in this
publication are entirely fictional. Any resemblance to actual persons (living or dead), events, or places, without
satirical intent, is coincidental. Printed in the USA. For international rights, contact:
foreignlicensing@imagecomics.com. ISBN: 978-1-5343-1644-7.

 Publication design by Sean Phillips

by Ed Brubaker and Sean Phillips

L P

Colors by Jacob Phillips

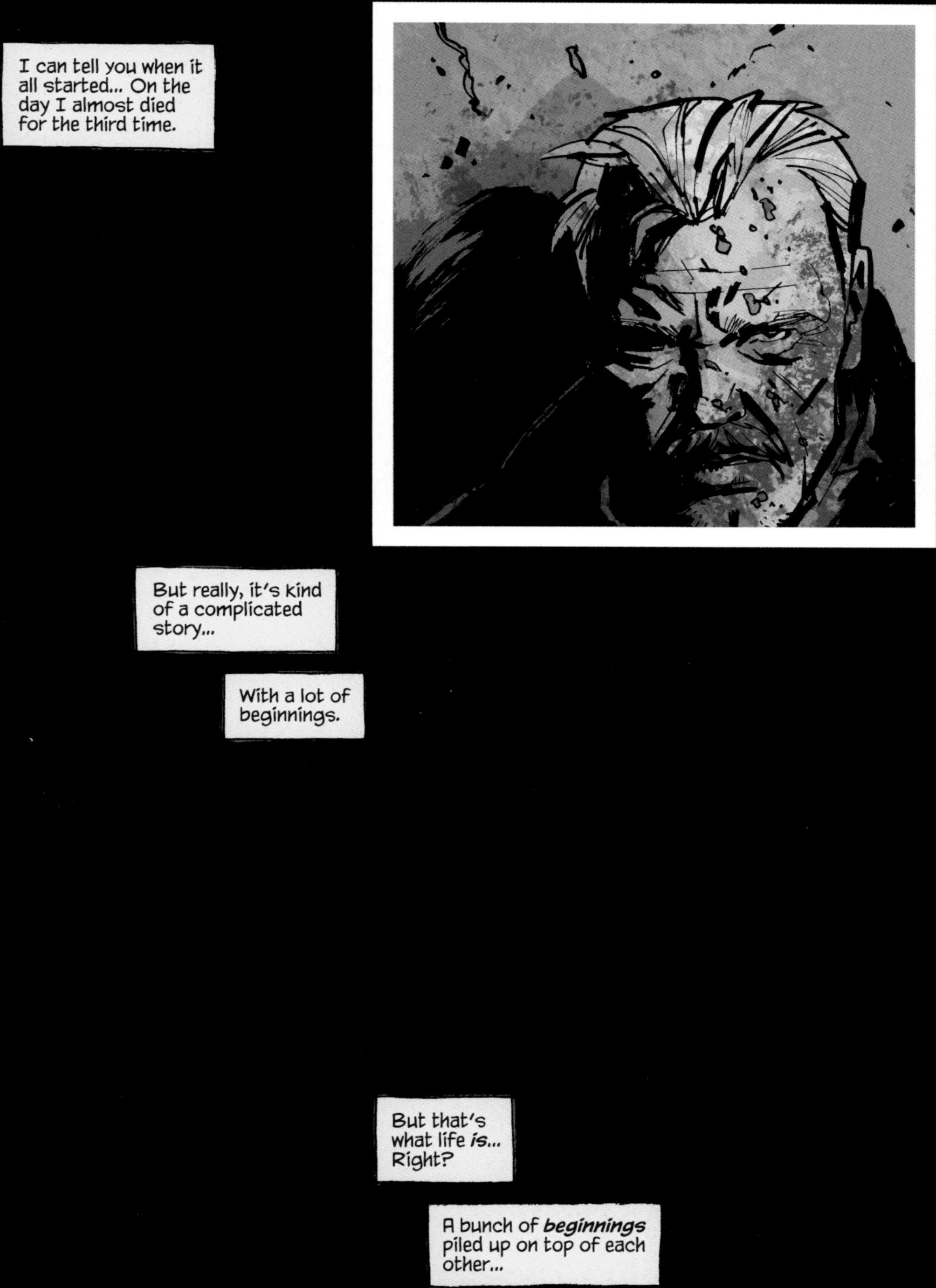
I can tell you when it all started... On the day I almost died for the third time.
But really, it's kind of a complicated story...
With a lot of beginnings.
But that's what life *is*... Right?
A bunch of ***beginnings*** piled up on top of each other...

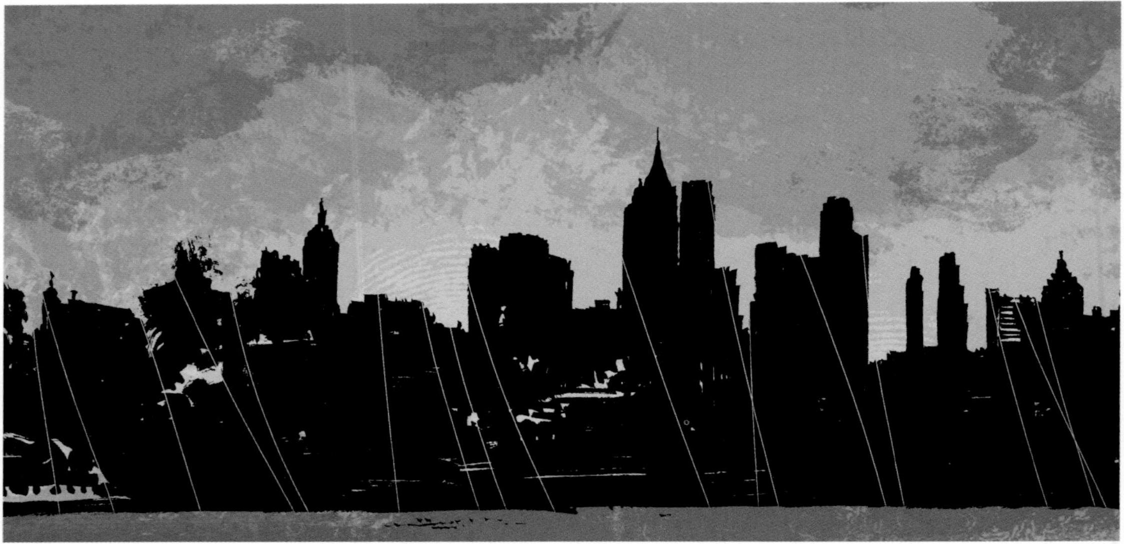

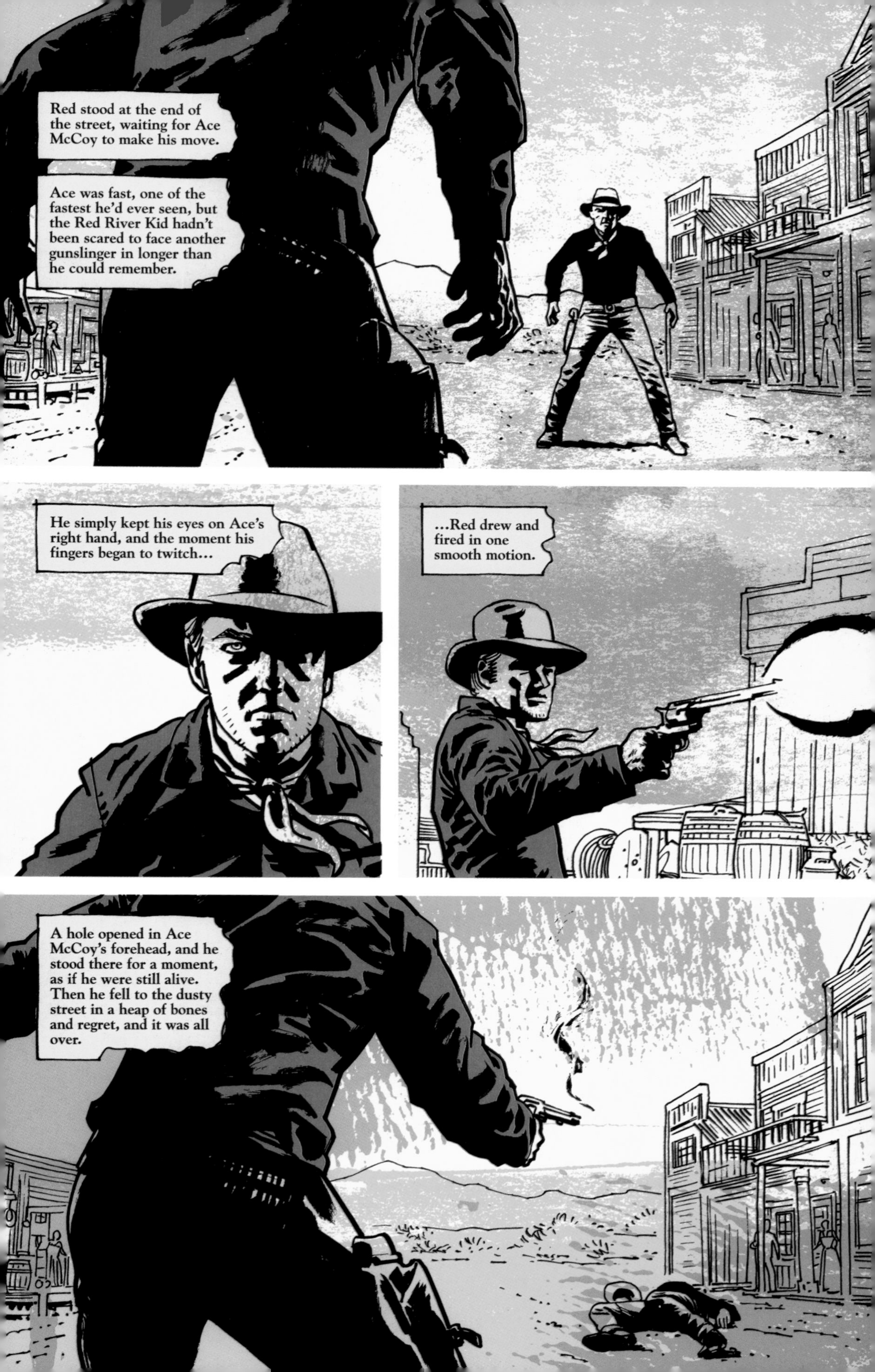
Red stood at the end of the street, waiting for Ace McCoy to make his move.
Ace was fast, one of the fastest he'd ever seen, but the Red River Kid hadn't been scared to face another gunslinger in longer than he could remember.
He simply kept his eyes on Ace's right hand, and the moment his fingers began to twitch...
...Red drew and fired in one smooth motion.
A hole opened in Ace McCoy's forehead, and he stood there for a moment, as if he were still alive. Then he fell to the dusty street in a heap of bones and regret, and it was all over.

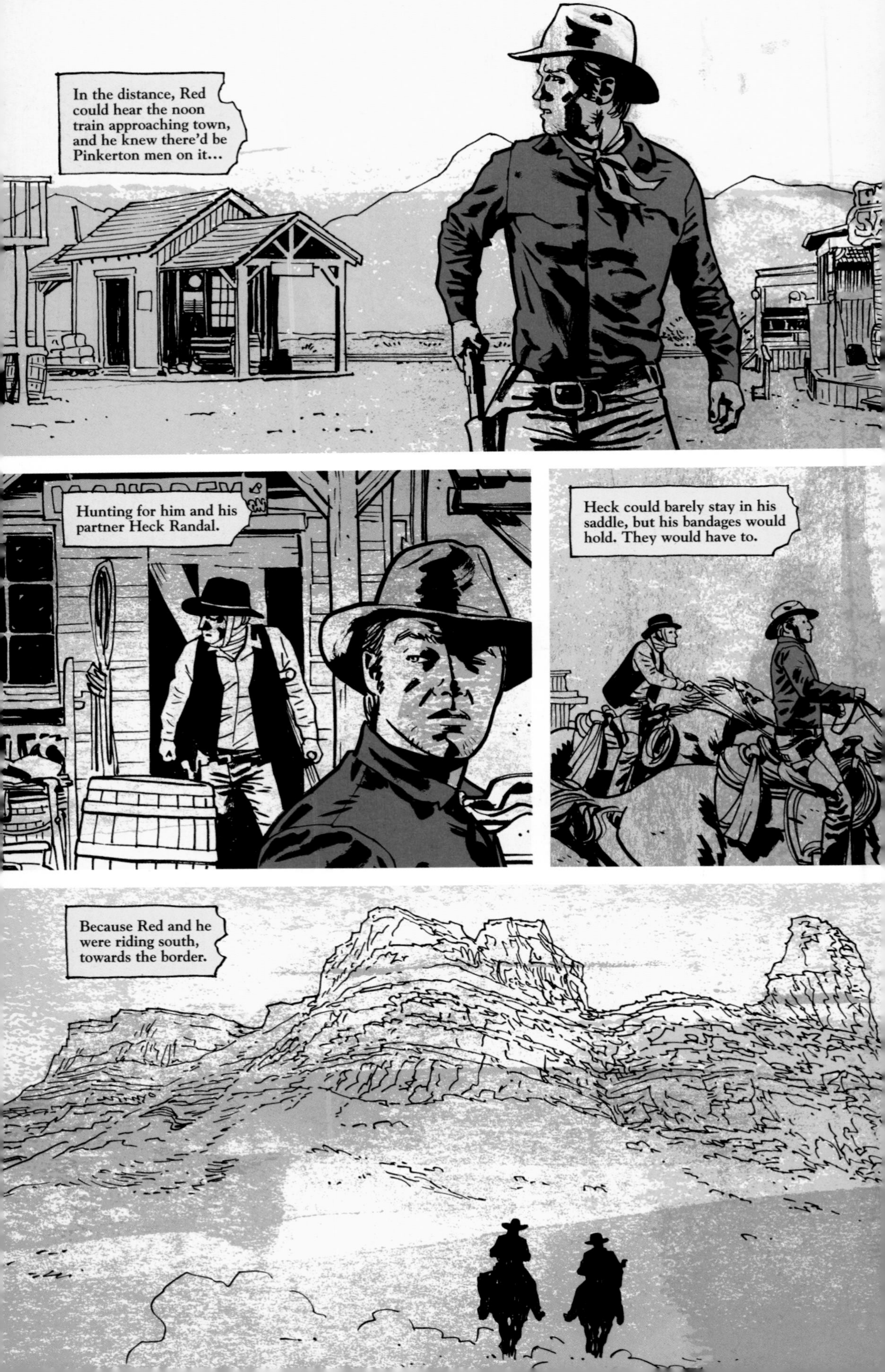
In the distance, Red could hear the noon train approaching town, and he knew there'd be Pinkerton men on it...
Hunting for him and his partner Heck Randal.
Heck could barely stay in his saddle, but his bandages would hold. They would have to.
Because Red and he were riding south, towards the border.

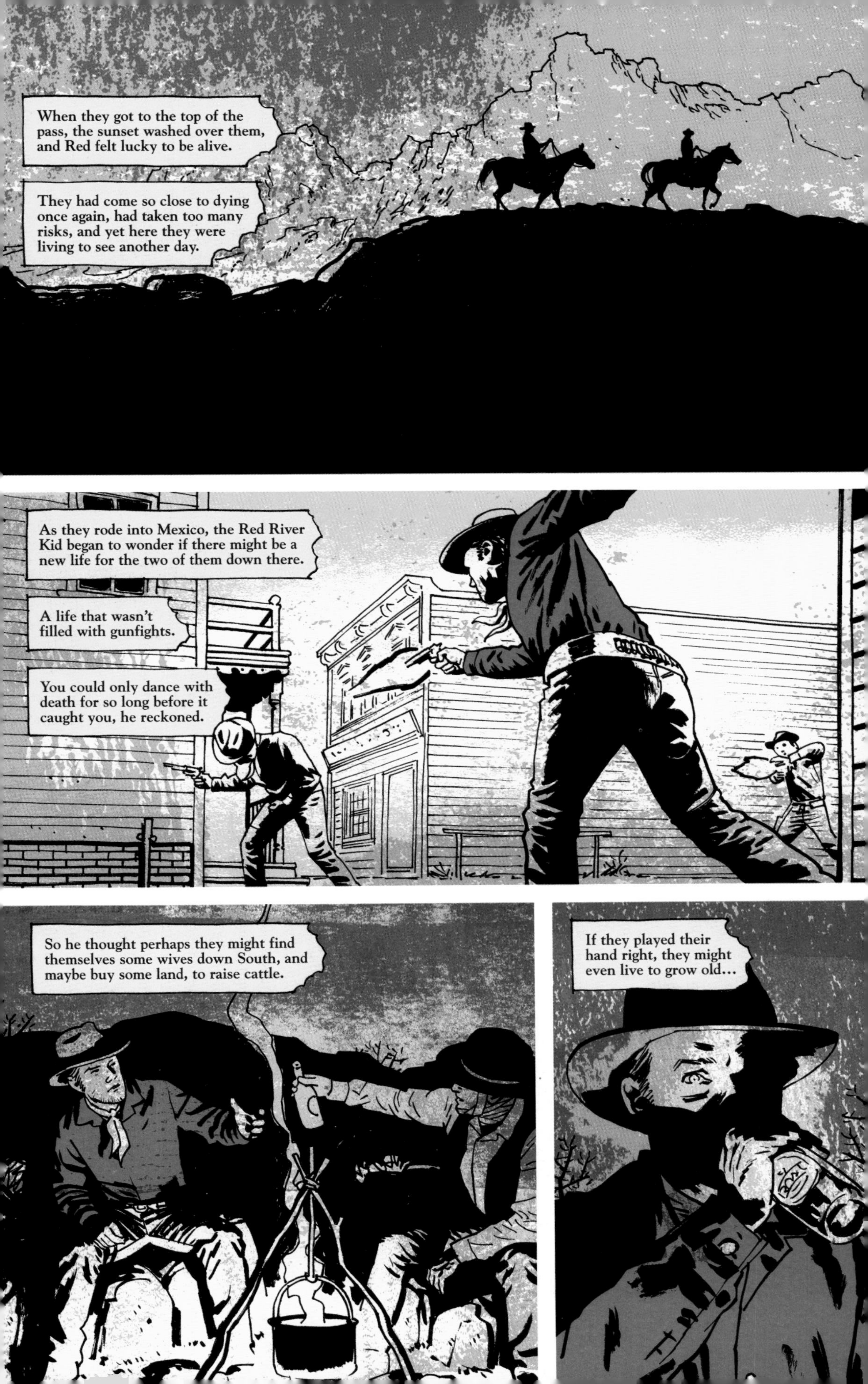

When they got to the top of the pass, the sunset washed over them, and Red felt lucky to be alive.
They had come so close to dying once again, had taken too many risks, and yet here they were living to see another day.
As they rode into Mexico, the Red River Kid began to wonder if there might be a new life for the two of them down there.
A life that wasn't filled with gunfights.
You could only dance with death for so long before it caught you, he reckoned.
So he thought perhaps they might find themselves some wives down South, and maybe buy some land, to raise cattle.
If they played their hand right, they might even live to grow old...

...Which so few gunslingers did.

...WHICH SO FEW GUNSLINGERS DID.

HNNH...

WHAT DO YOU THINK?

IT'S GOOD STUFF, MAX...

JUST NEED TO FIX THIS ENDING.

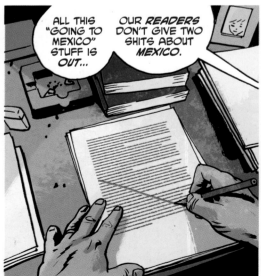

ALL THIS "GOING TO MEXICO" STUFF IS OUT...

OUR READERS DON'T GIVE TWO SHITS ABOUT MEXICO.

AN' IT SOUNDS LIKE YOU'VE GOT RED AND HECK RETIRING HERE, MAX.

NO... NOT EXACTLY...

BUT I WANT TO DO SOME STORIES ABOUT THEIR *LATER* YEARS... SHOW THEIR LIVES AS MORE OF A *TAPESTRY*.

NOT JUST THE SAME *SHOOT 'EM UPS* EVERY ISSUE.

THE MAG IS CALLED *SIX GUN WESTERN*, MAX.

OUR READERS *WANT* THE SHOOT 'EM UPS.

WINTER
10¢
SIX GUN
western
A Brand New Book-Length Novel
RUSTLERS OF WEST FORK
By Max Winters

HOWARD DID THIS EXACT THING WITH *CONAN* AND NO ONE COMPLAINED.

SOMETIMES HE'S *OLD*... SOMETIMES HE'S *YOUNG*...

YEAH, BUT HE'S NEVER A FUCKIN' *FARMER* IN *MEXICO*, IS HE?

FORGET IT, MAX... JUST STICK TO THE *FORMULA*...

RED AND HECK HELP SOME PRAIRIE FOLK OR *WHOEVER*...

THEY SHOOT SOME *BAD GUYS*...

AN' THEN THEY RIDE OFF TO THE *NEXT* ADVENTURE.

THAT'S WHAT PAYS THE *BILLS*.

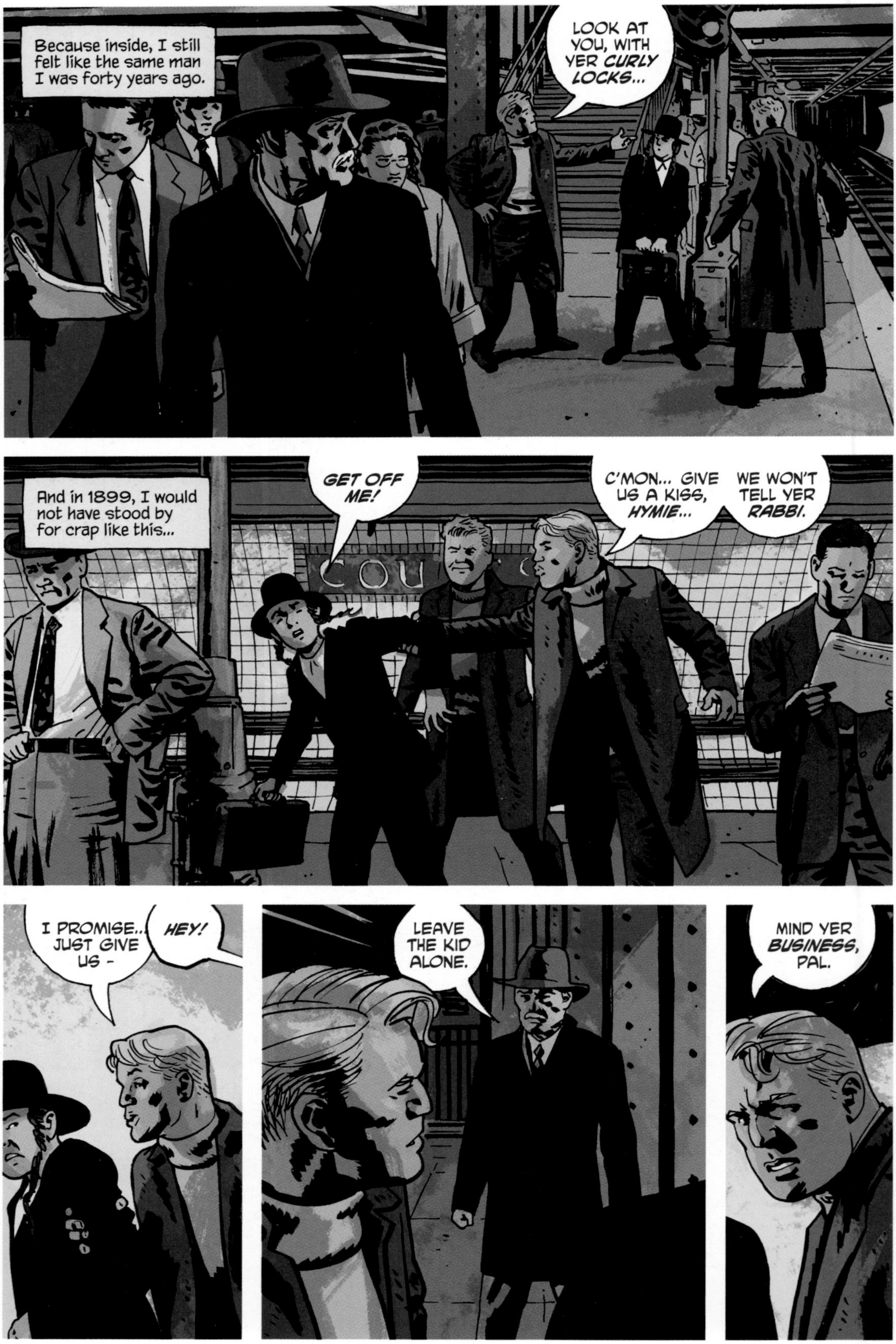
Because inside, I still felt like the same man I was forty years ago.
LOOK AT YOU, WITH YER CURLY LOCKS...
And in 1899, I would not have stood by for crap like this...
GET OFF ME!
C'MON... GIVE US A KISS, HYMIE...
WE WON'T TELL YER RABBI.
I PROMISE... JUST GIVE US -
HEY!
LEAVE THE KID ALONE.
MIND YER BUSINESS, PAL.

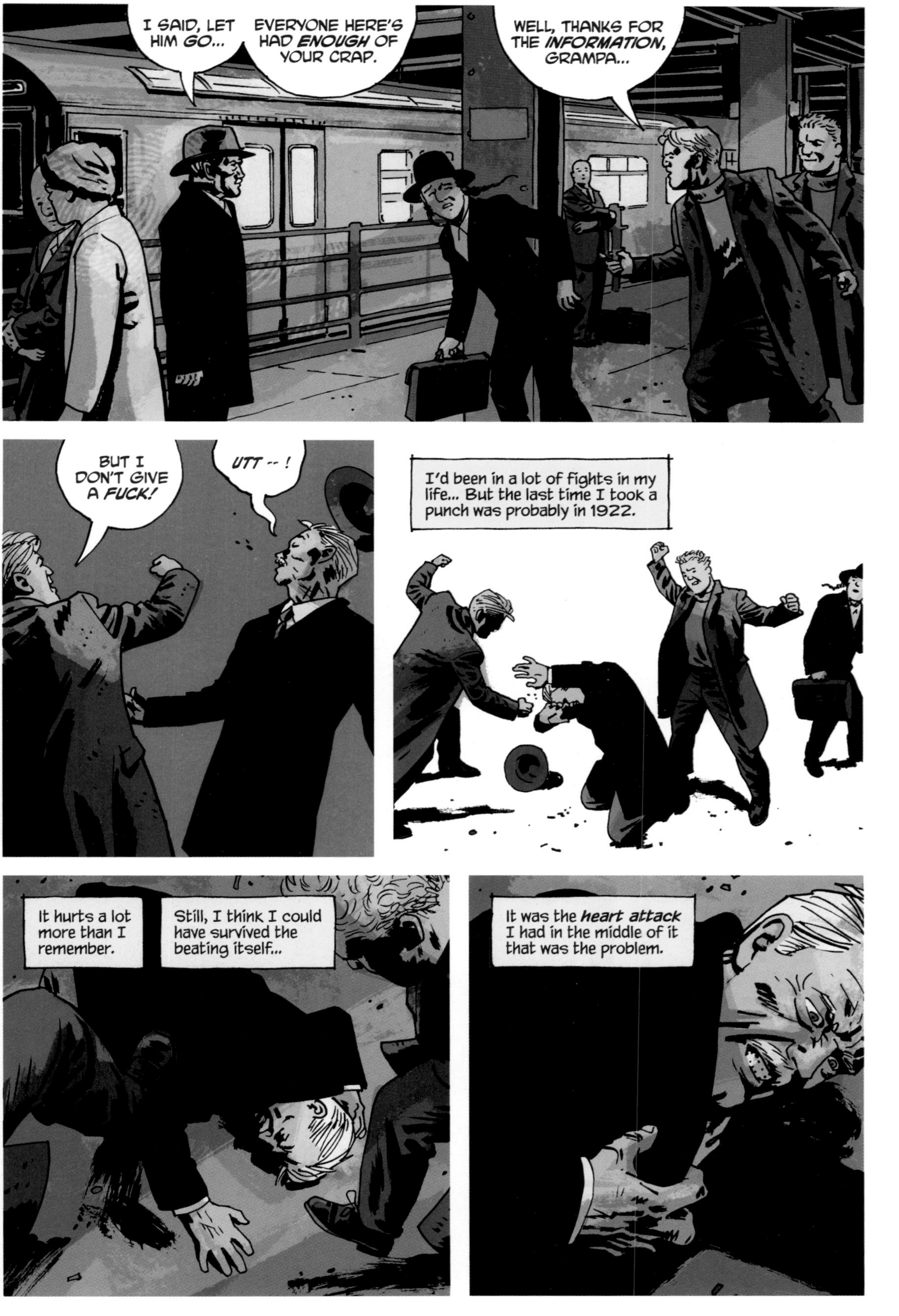

I SAID, LET HIM GO...
EVERYONE HERE'S HAD ENOUGH OF YOUR CRAP.
WELL, THANKS FOR THE INFORMATION, GRAMPA...
BUT I DON'T GIVE A FUCK!
UTT -- !
I'd been in a lot of fights in my life... But the last time I took a punch was probably in 1922.
It hurts a lot more than I remember.
Still, I think I could have survived the beating itself...
It was the heart attack I had in the middle of it that was the problem.

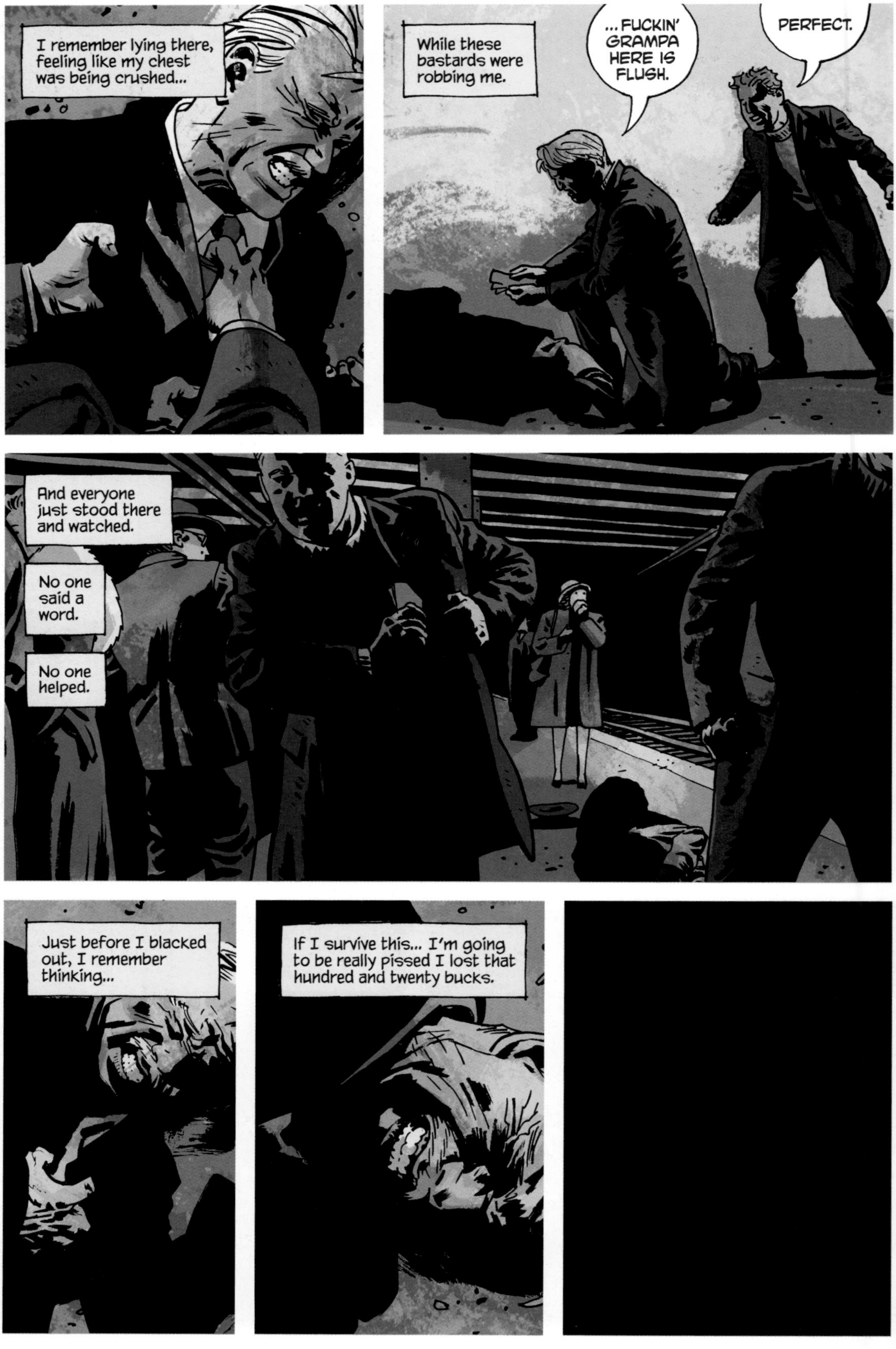

I remember lying there, feeling like my chest was being crushed...
While these bastards were robbing me.
...FUCKIN' GRAMPA HERE IS FLUSH.
PERFECT.
And everyone just stood there and watched.
No one said a word.
No one helped.
Just before I blacked out, I remember thinking...
If I survive this... I'm going to be really pissed I lost that hundred and twenty bucks.

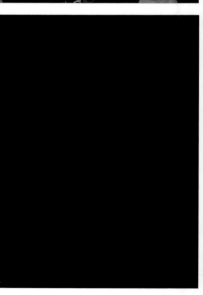

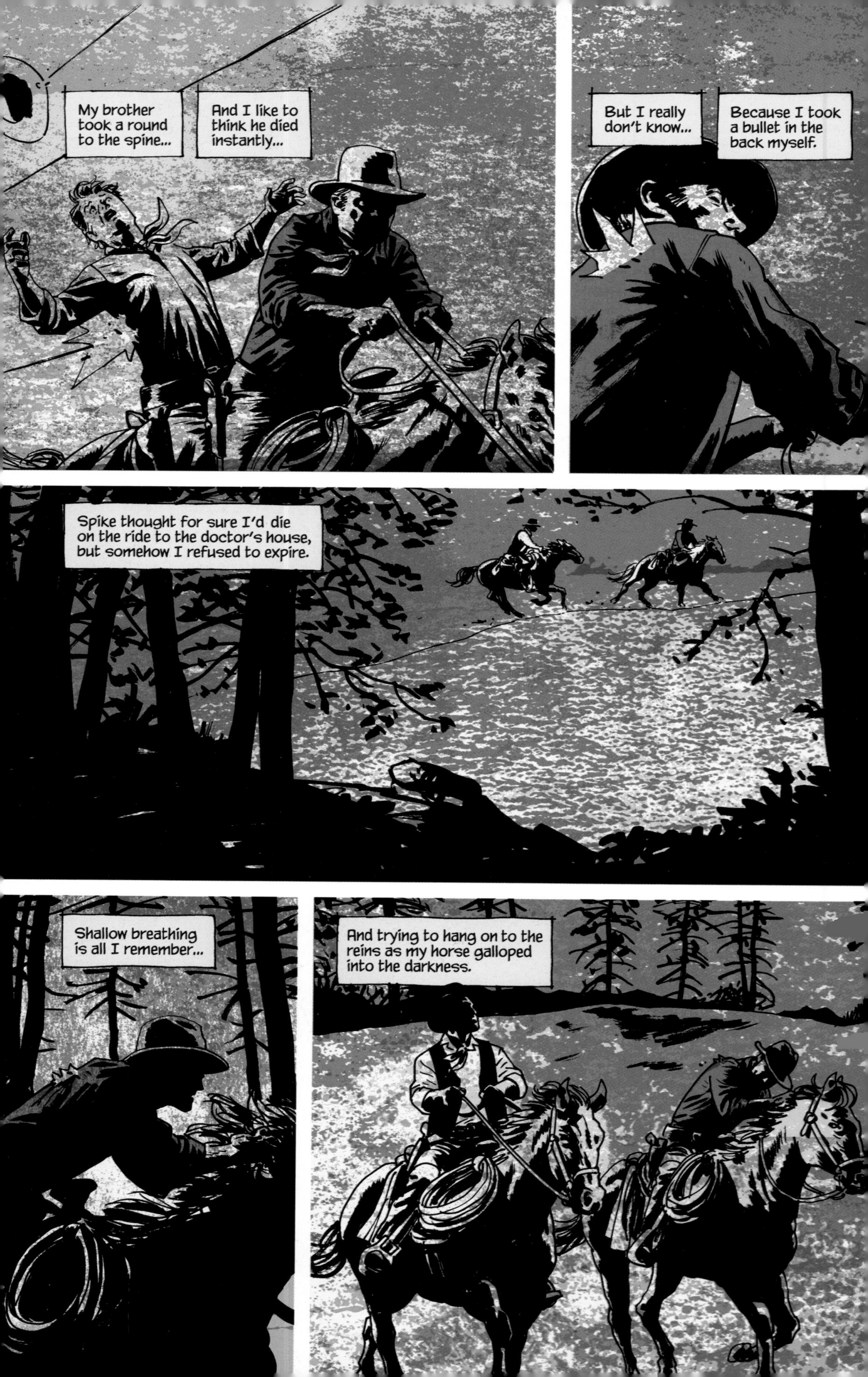
My brother took a round to the spine...
And I like to think he died instantly...
But I really don't know...
Because I took a bullet in the back myself.
Spike thought for sure I'd die on the ride to the doctor's house, but somehow I refused to expire.
Shallow breathing is all I remember...
And trying to hang on to the reins as my horse galloped into the darkness.

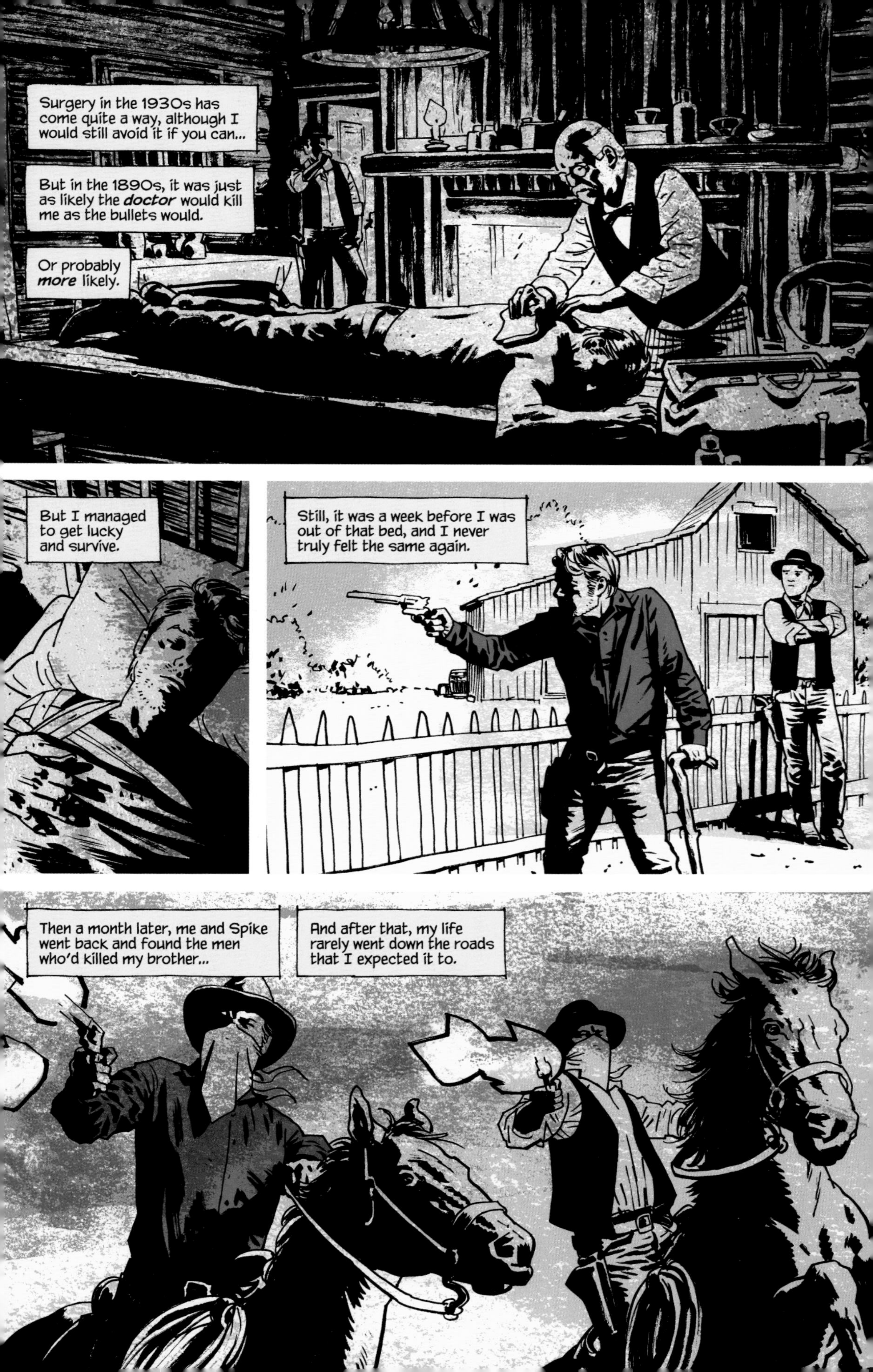
Surgery in the 1930s has come quite a way, although I would still avoid it if you can...
But in the 1890s, it was just as likely the *doctor* would kill me as the bullets would.
Or probably *more* likely.
But I managed to get lucky and survive.
Still, it was a week before I was out of that bed, and I never truly felt the same again.
Then a month later, me and Spike went back and found the men who'd killed my brother...
And after that, my life rarely went down the roads that I expected it to.

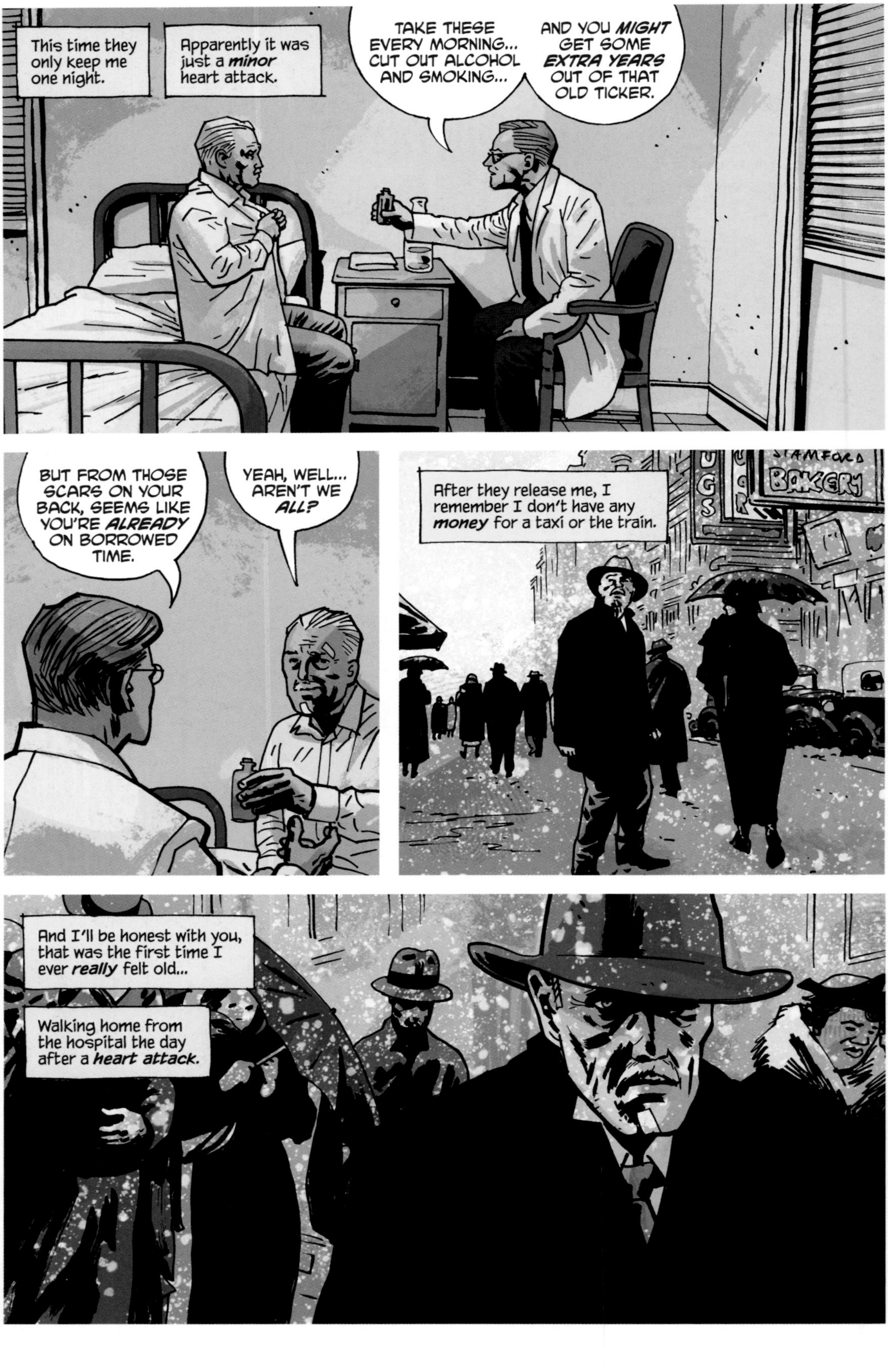
This time they only keep me one night.
Apparently it was just a minor heart attack.
TAKE THESE EVERY MORNING... CUT OUT ALCOHOL AND SMOKING...
AND YOU MIGHT GET SOME EXTRA YEARS OUT OF THAT OLD TICKER.
BUT FROM THOSE SCARS ON YOUR BACK, SEEMS LIKE YOU'RE ALREADY ON BORROWED TIME.
YEAH, WELL... AREN'T WE ALL?
After they release me, I remember I don't have any money for a taxi or the train.
BAKERY
And I'll be honest with you, that was the first time I ever really felt old...
Walking home from the hospital the day after a heart attack.

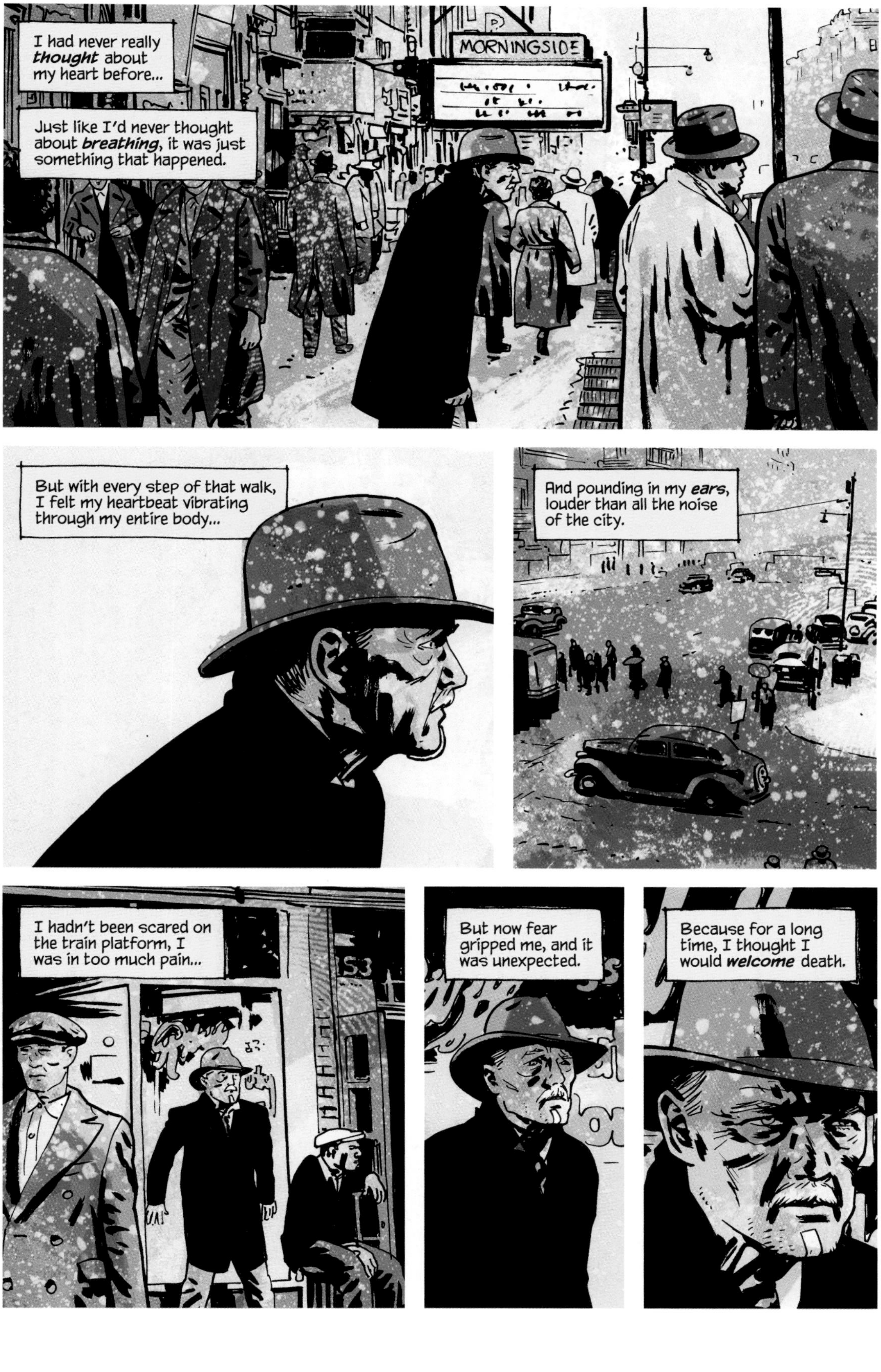
MORNINGSIDE
I had never really *thought* about my heart before...
Just like I'd never thought about *breathing*, it was just something that happened.
But with every step of that walk, I felt my heartbeat vibrating through my entire body...
And pounding in my *ears*, louder than all the noise of the city.
I hadn't been scared on the train platform, I was in too much pain...
But now fear gripped me, and it was unexpected.
Because for a long time, I thought I would *welcome* death.

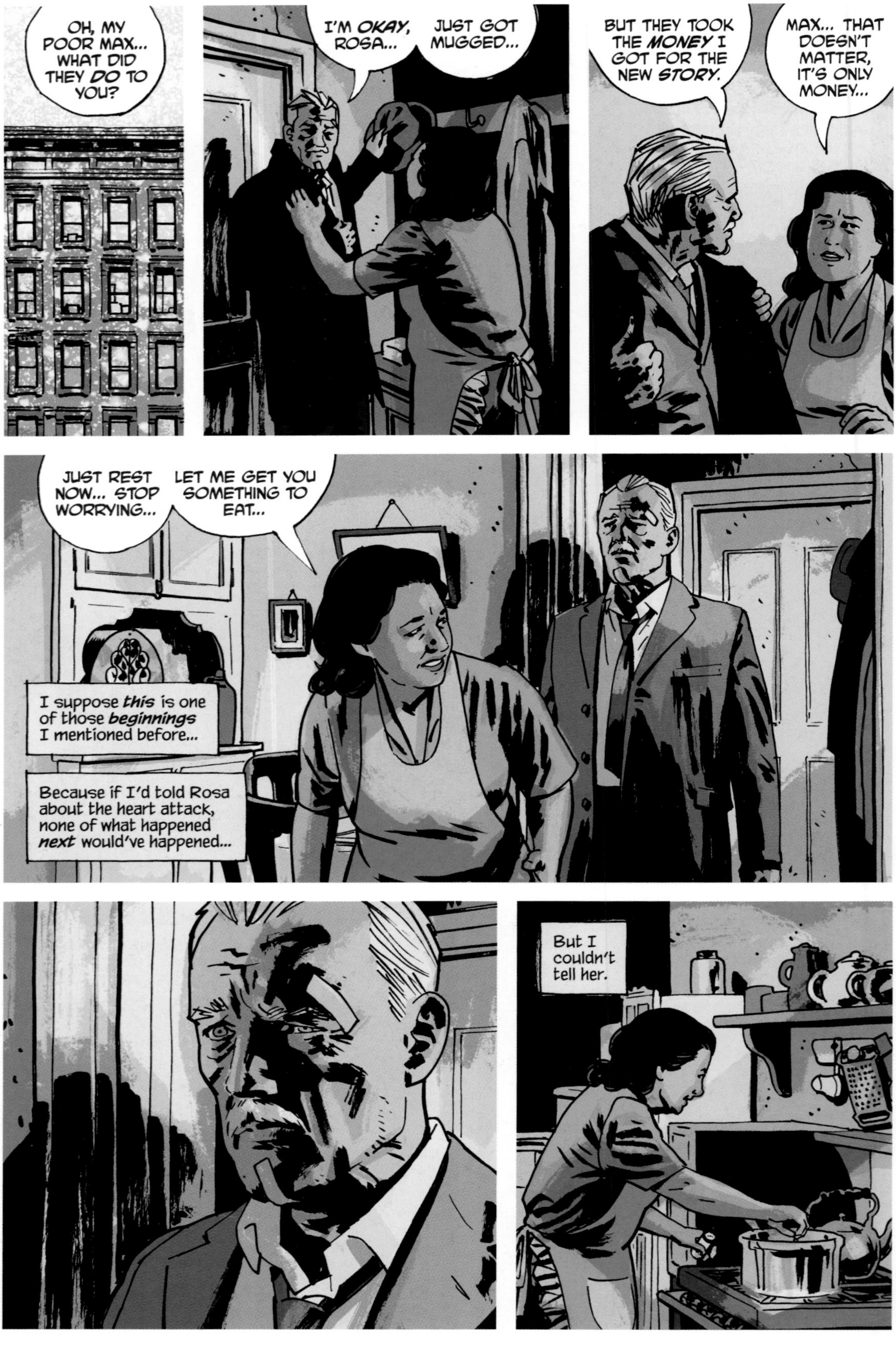
OH, MY POOR MAX... WHAT DID THEY DO TO YOU?
I'M OKAY, ROSA...
JUST GOT MUGGED...
BUT THEY TOOK THE MONEY I GOT FOR THE NEW STORY.
MAX... THAT DOESN'T MATTER, IT'S ONLY MONEY...
JUST REST NOW... STOP WORRYING...
LET ME GET YOU SOMETHING TO EAT...
I suppose this is one of those beginnings I mentioned before...
Because if I'd told Rosa about the heart attack, none of what happened next would've happened...
But I couldn't tell her.

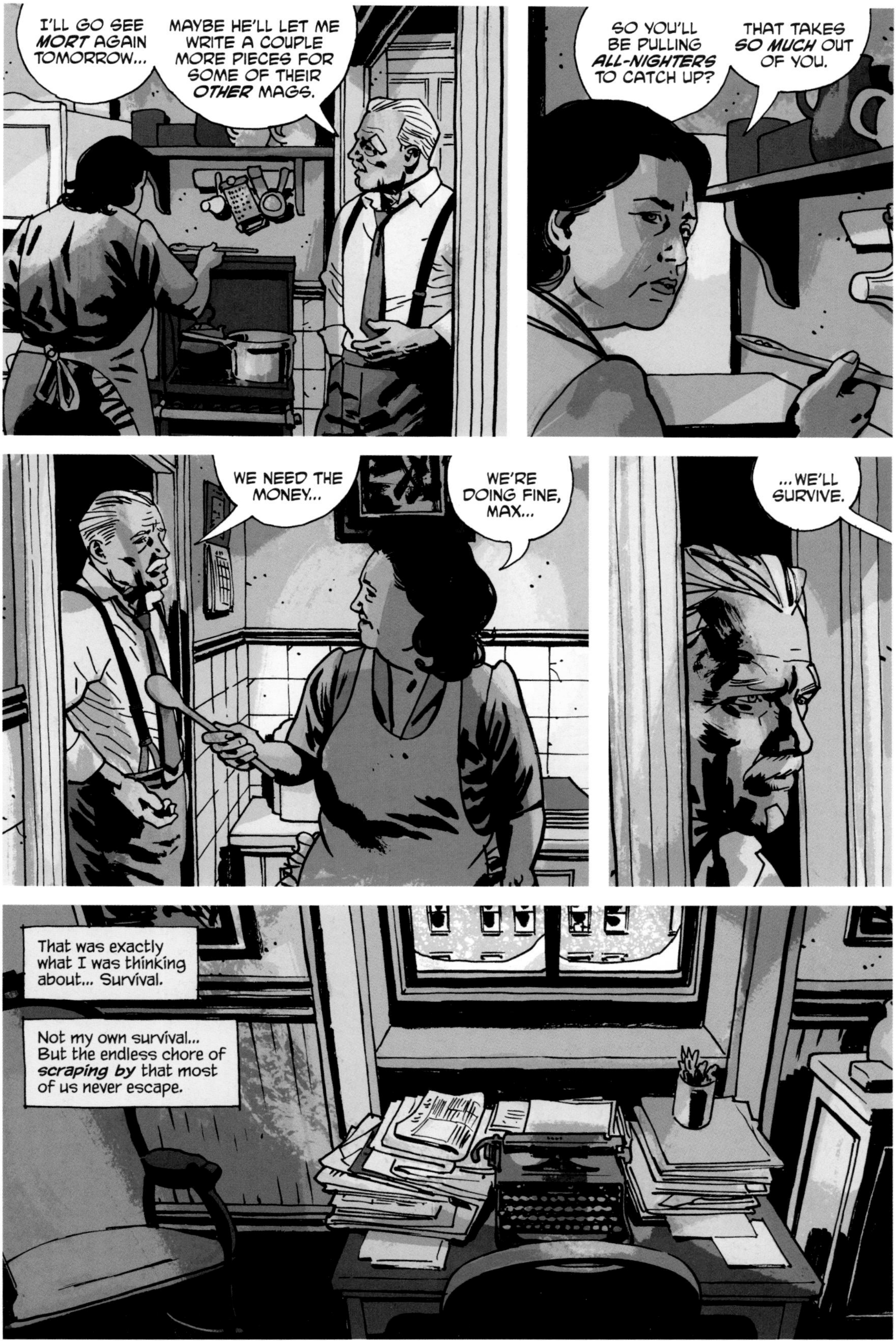
I'LL GO SEE *MORT* AGAIN TOMORROW...
MAYBE HE'LL LET ME WRITE A COUPLE MORE PIECES FOR SOME OF THEIR *OTHER* MAGS.
SO YOU'LL BE PULLING *ALL-NIGHTERS* TO CATCH UP?
THAT TAKES *SO MUCH* OUT OF YOU.
WE NEED THE MONEY...
WE'RE DOING FINE, MAX...
...WE'LL SURVIVE.
That was exactly what I was thinking about... Survival.
Not my own survival... But the endless chore of *scraping by* that most of us never escape.

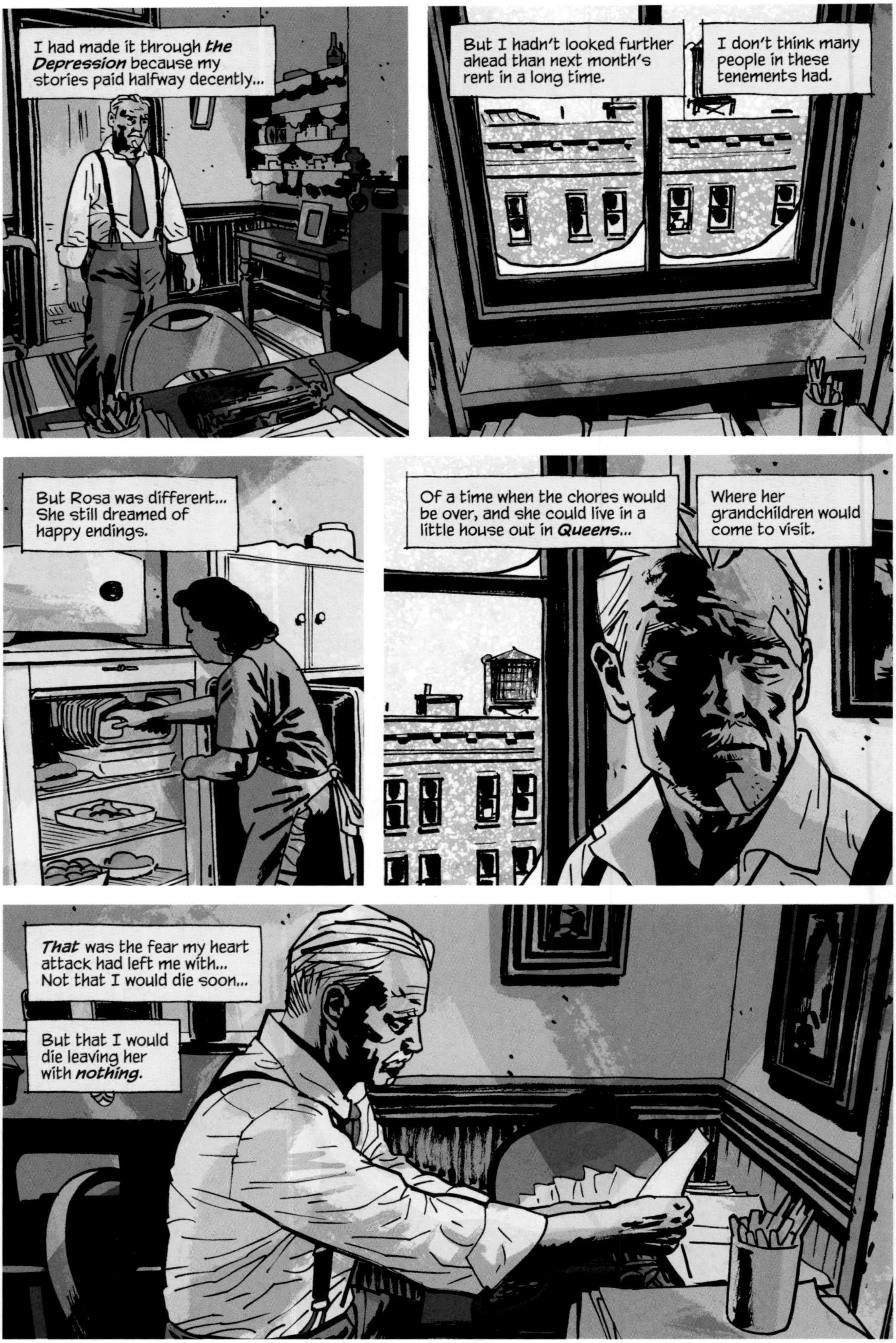
I had made it through *the Depression* because my stories paid halfway decently...
But I hadn't looked further ahead than next month's rent in a long time.
I don't think many people in these tenements had.
But Rosa was different... She still dreamed of happy endings.
Of a time when the chores would be over, and she could live in a little house out in *Queens*...
Where her grandchildren would come to visit.
That was the fear my heart attack had left me with... Not that I would die soon...
But that I would die leaving her with *nothing*.

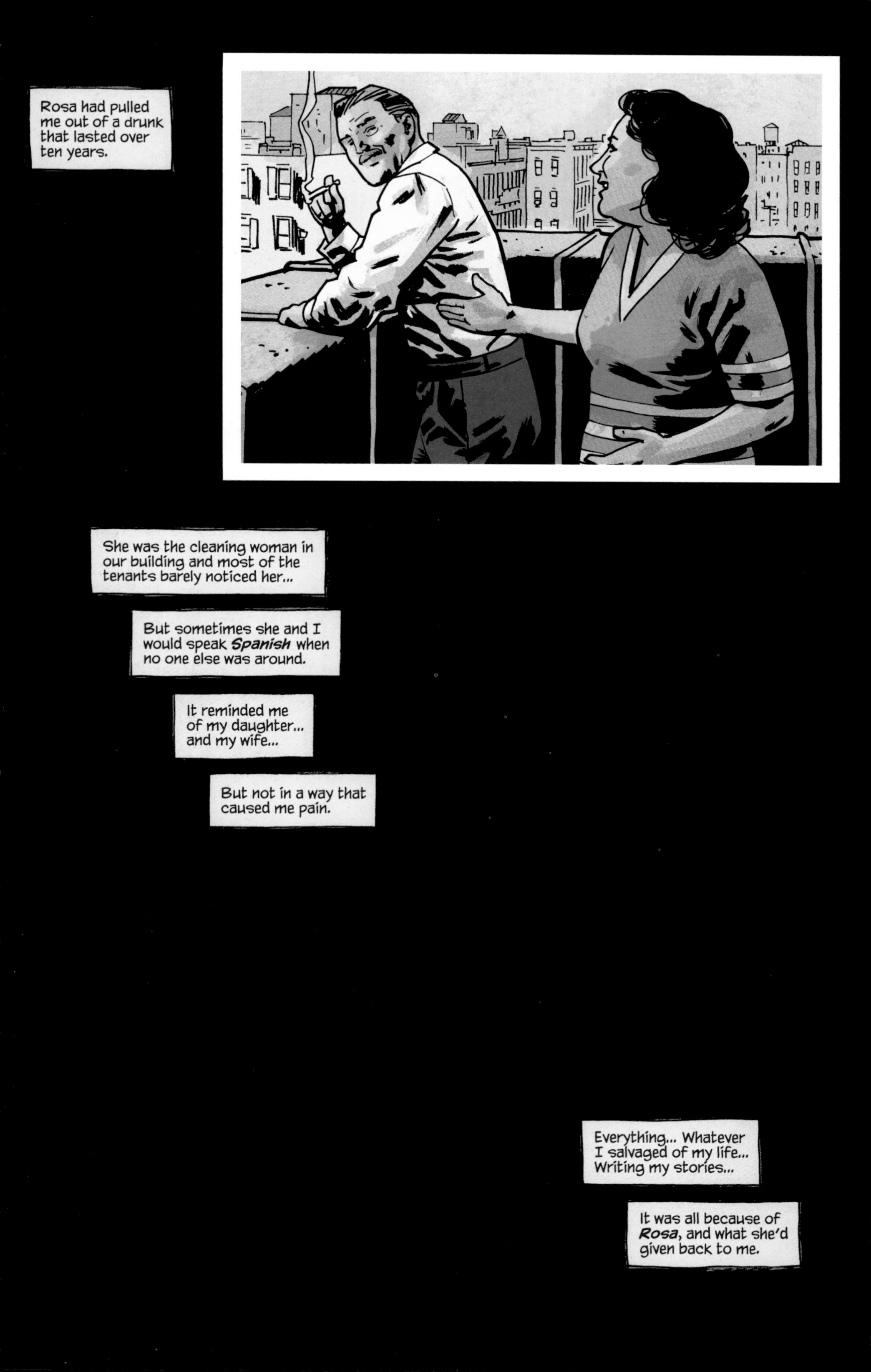
Rosa had pulled me out of a drunk that lasted over ten years.
She was the cleaning woman in our building and most of the tenants barely noticed her...
But sometimes she and I would speak *Spanish* when no one else was around.
It reminded me of my daughter... and my wife...
But not in a way that caused me pain.
Everything... Whatever I salvaged of my life... Writing my stories...
It was all because of *Rosa*, and what she'd given back to me.

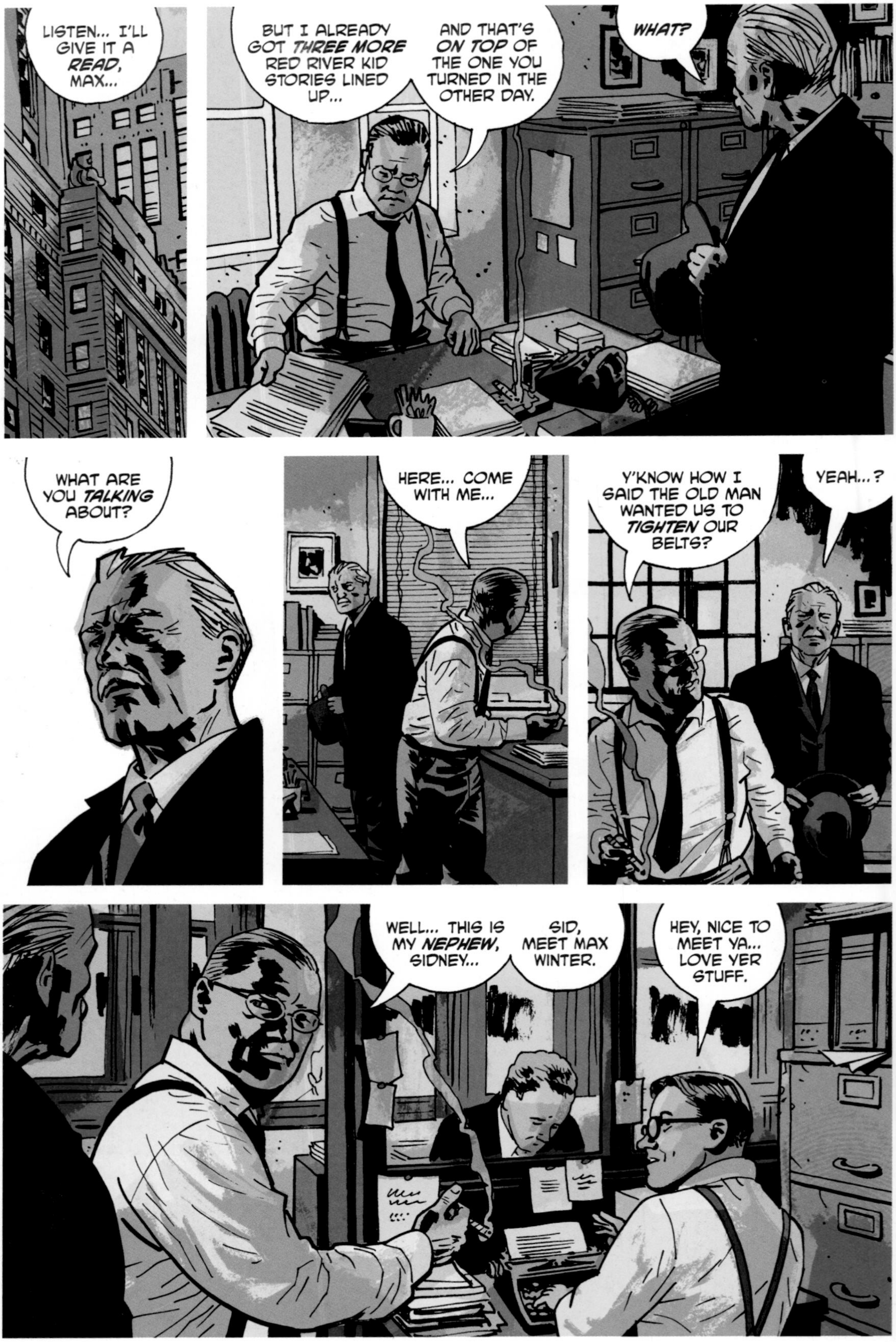
LISTEN... I'LL GIVE IT A *READ,* MAX...
BUT I ALREADY GOT *THREE MORE* RED RIVER KID STORIES LINED UP...
AND THAT'S *ON TOP* OF THE ONE YOU TURNED IN THE OTHER DAY.
WHAT?
WHAT ARE YOU *TALKING* ABOUT?
HERE... COME WITH ME...
Y'KNOW HOW I SAID THE OLD MAN WANTED US TO *TIGHTEN* OUR BELTS?
YEAH...?
WELL... THIS IS MY *NEPHEW,* SIDNEY...
SID, MEET MAX WINTER.
HEY, NICE TO MEET YA... LOVE YER STUFF.

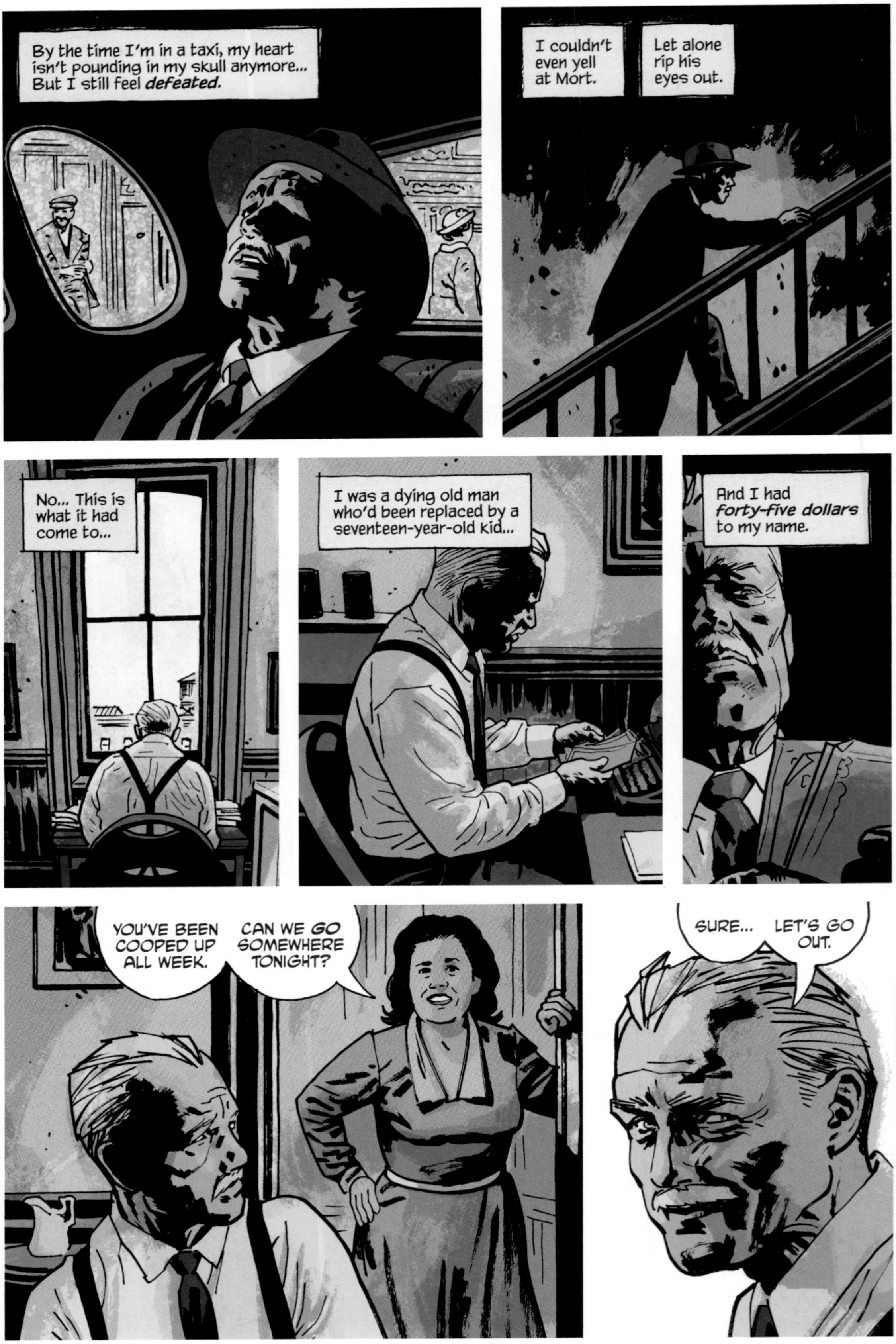

By the time I'm in a taxi, my heart isn't pounding in my skull anymore... But I still feel *defeated.*
I couldn't even yell at Mort.
Let alone rip his eyes out.
No... This is what it had come to...
I was a dying old man who'd been replaced by a seventeen-year-old kid...
And I had *forty-five dollars* to my name.
YOU'VE BEEN COOPED UP ALL WEEK.
CAN WE *GO* SOMEWHERE TONIGHT?
SURE...
LET'S GO OUT.

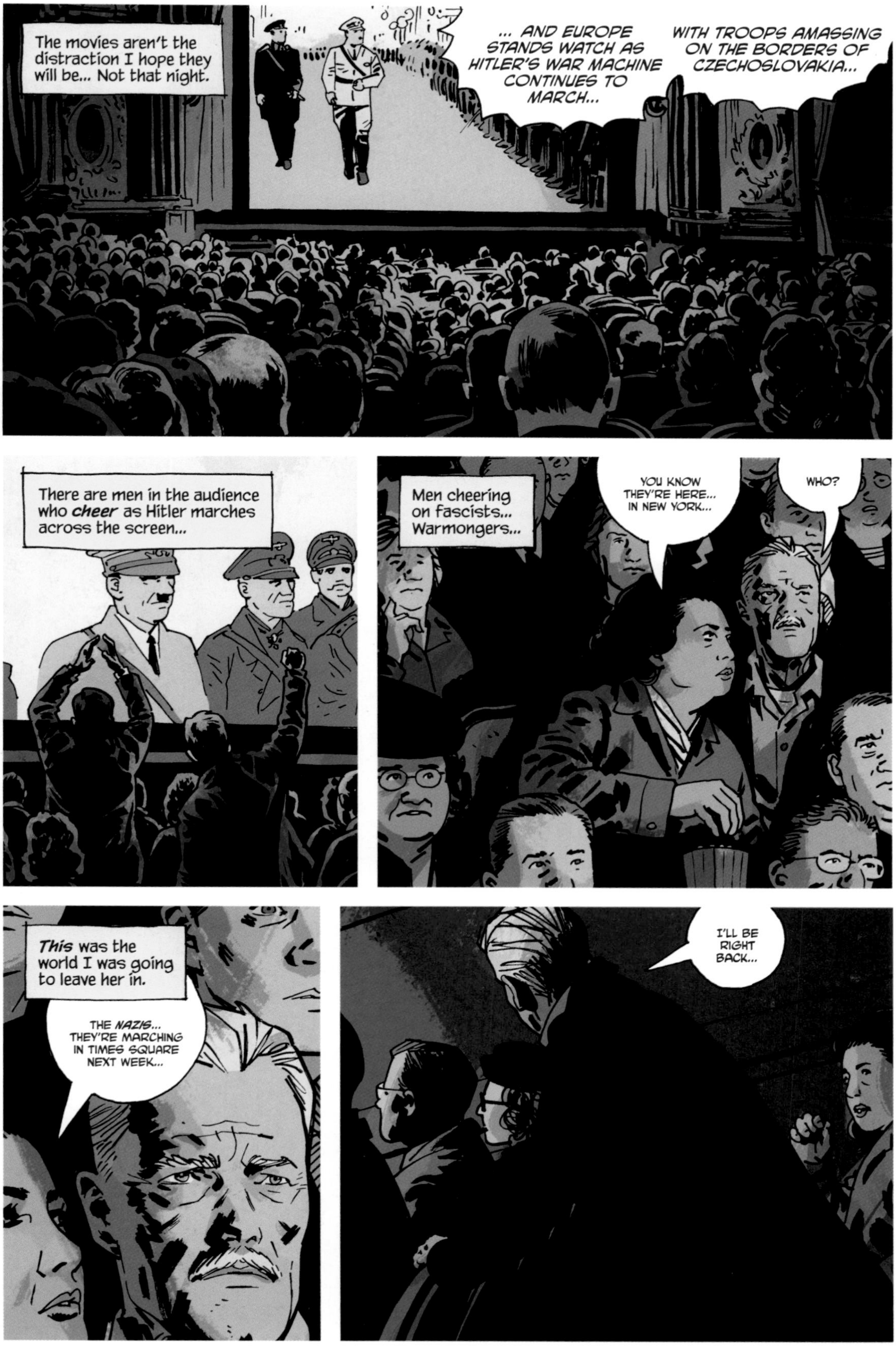
The movies aren't the distraction I hope they will be... Not that night.
... AND EUROPE STANDS WATCH AS HITLER'S WAR MACHINE CONTINUES TO MARCH...
WITH TROOPS AMASSING ON THE BORDERS OF CZECHOSLOVAKIA...
There are men in the audience who *cheer* as Hitler marches across the screen...
Men cheering on fascists... Warmongers...
YOU KNOW THEY'RE HERE... IN NEW YORK...
WHO?
This was the world I was going to leave her in.
THE *NAZIS*... THEY'RE MARCHING IN TIMES SQUARE NEXT WEEK...
I'LL BE RIGHT BACK...

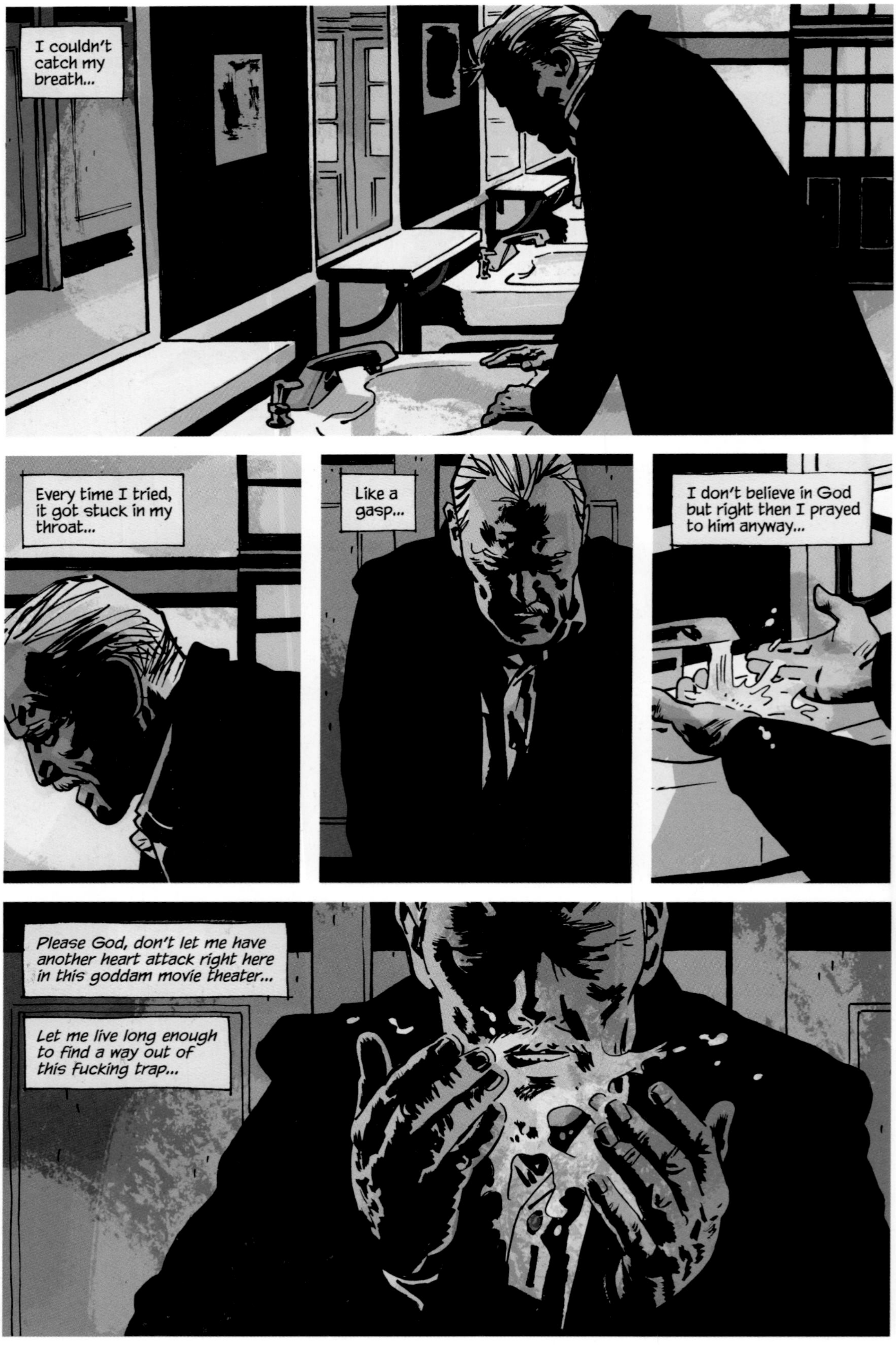
I couldn't catch my breath...
Every time I tried, it got stuck in my throat...
Like a gasp...
I don't believe in God but right then I prayed to him anyway...
Please God, don't let me have another heart attack right here in this goddam movie theater...
Let me live long enough to find a way out of this fucking trap...

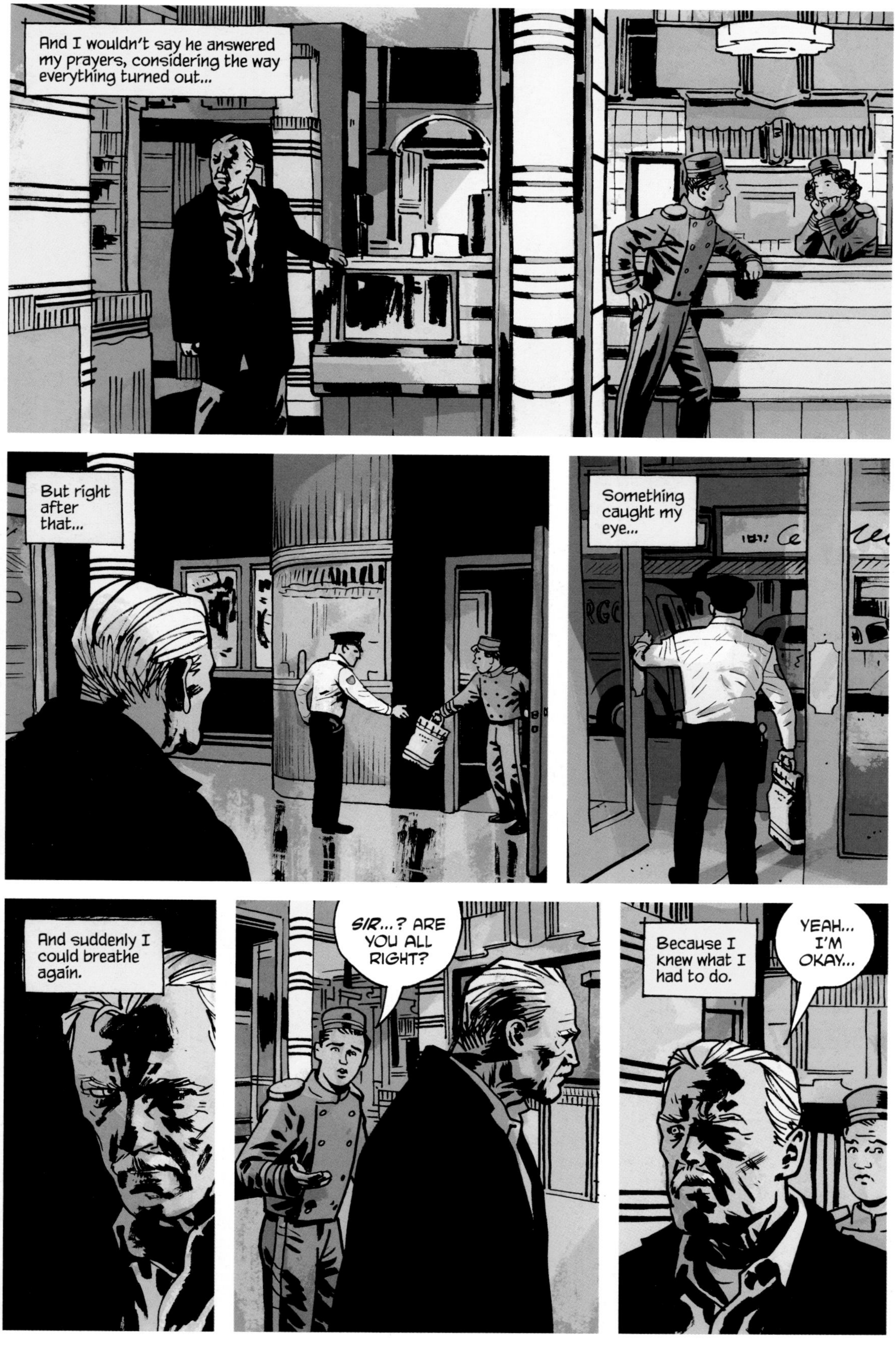

And I wouldn't say he answered my prayers, considering the way everything turned out...
But right after that...
Something caught my eye...
And suddenly I could breathe again.
SIR...? ARE YOU ALL RIGHT?
Because I knew what I had to do.
YEAH... I'M OKAY...

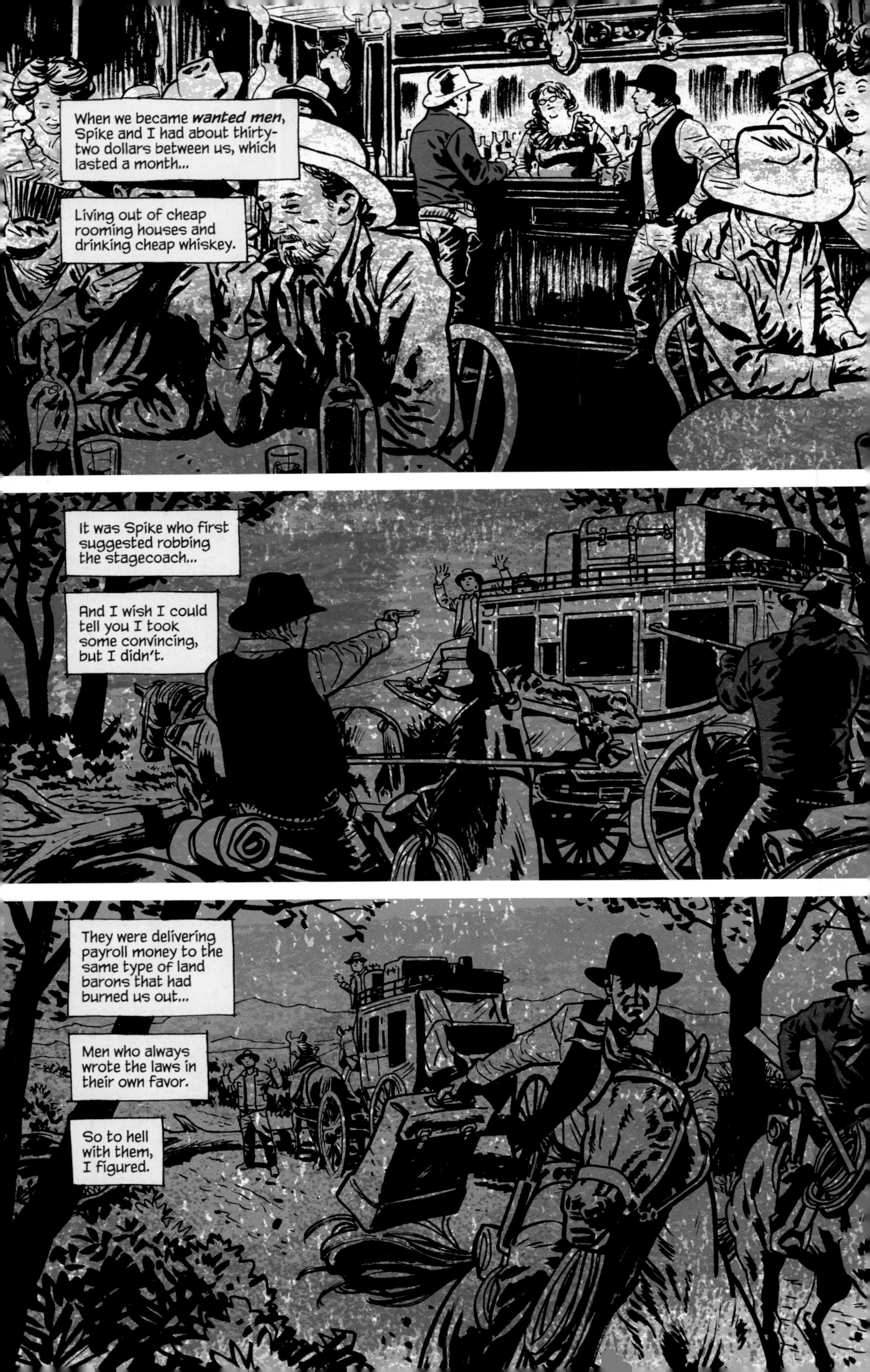

When we became ***wanted men***, Spike and I had about thirty-two dollars between us, which lasted a month...
Living out of cheap rooming houses and drinking cheap whiskey.
It was Spike who first suggested robbing the stagecoach...
And I wish I could tell you I took some convincing, but I didn't.
They were delivering payroll money to the same type of land barons that had burned us out...
Men who always wrote the laws in their own favor.
So to hell with them, I figured.

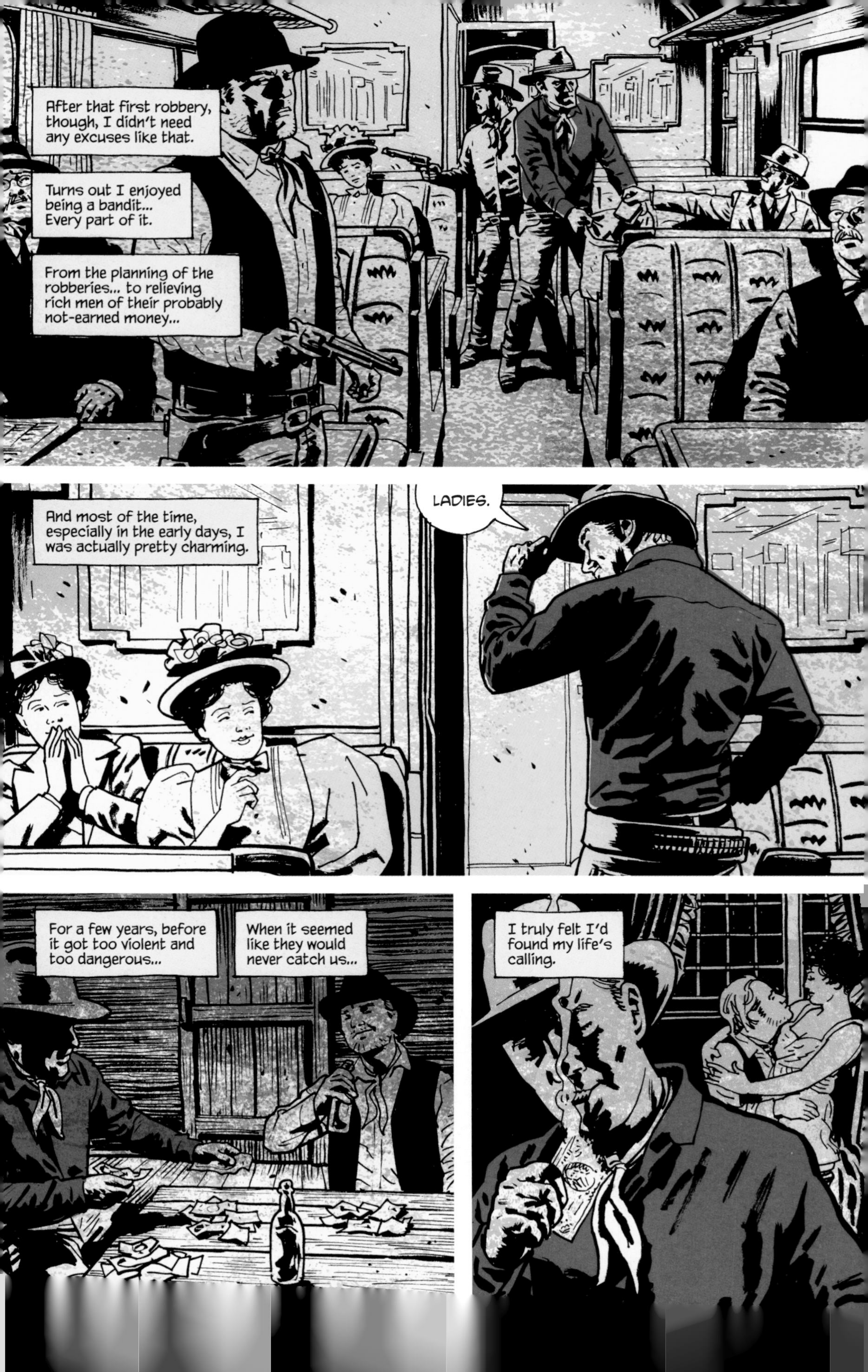
After that first robbery, though, I didn't need any excuses like that.
Turns out I enjoyed being a bandit... Every part of it.
From the planning of the robberies... to relieving rich men of their probably not-earned money...
And most of the time, especially in the early days, I was actually pretty charming.
LADIES.
For a few years, before it got too violent and too dangerous...
When it seemed like they would never catch us...
I truly felt I'd found my life's calling.

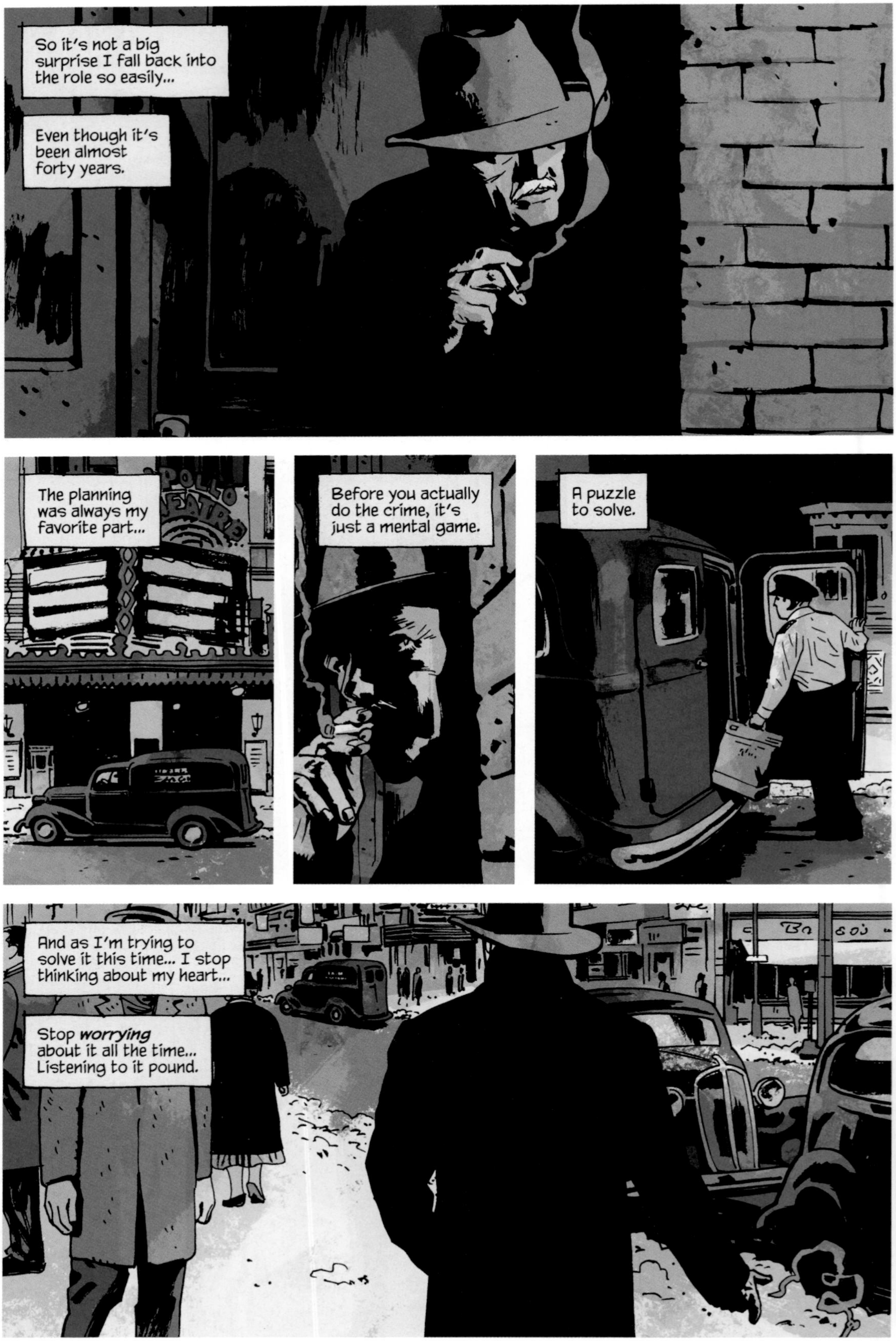
So it's not a big surprise I fall back into the role so easily...
Even though it's been almost forty years.
The planning was always my favorite part...
Before you actually do the crime, it's just a mental game.
A puzzle to solve.
And as I'm trying to solve it this time... I stop thinking about my heart...
Stop *worrying* about it all the time... Listening to it pound.

I'm just following the armored truck from the bank as it winds through the neighborhood.

Tracking its routine. Making mental notes.

The guards are lazy, they've been doing this job for years with no trouble.

LONDON CHEMISTS

The *driver* doesn't even get out to watch the back door during pick-ups.

MARCH SPICY PIRATE STORIES

After four days, I have a *halfway decent* plan.

Which, for a robbery I'm doing without any partners...

... Is *probably* as good as it's going to get.

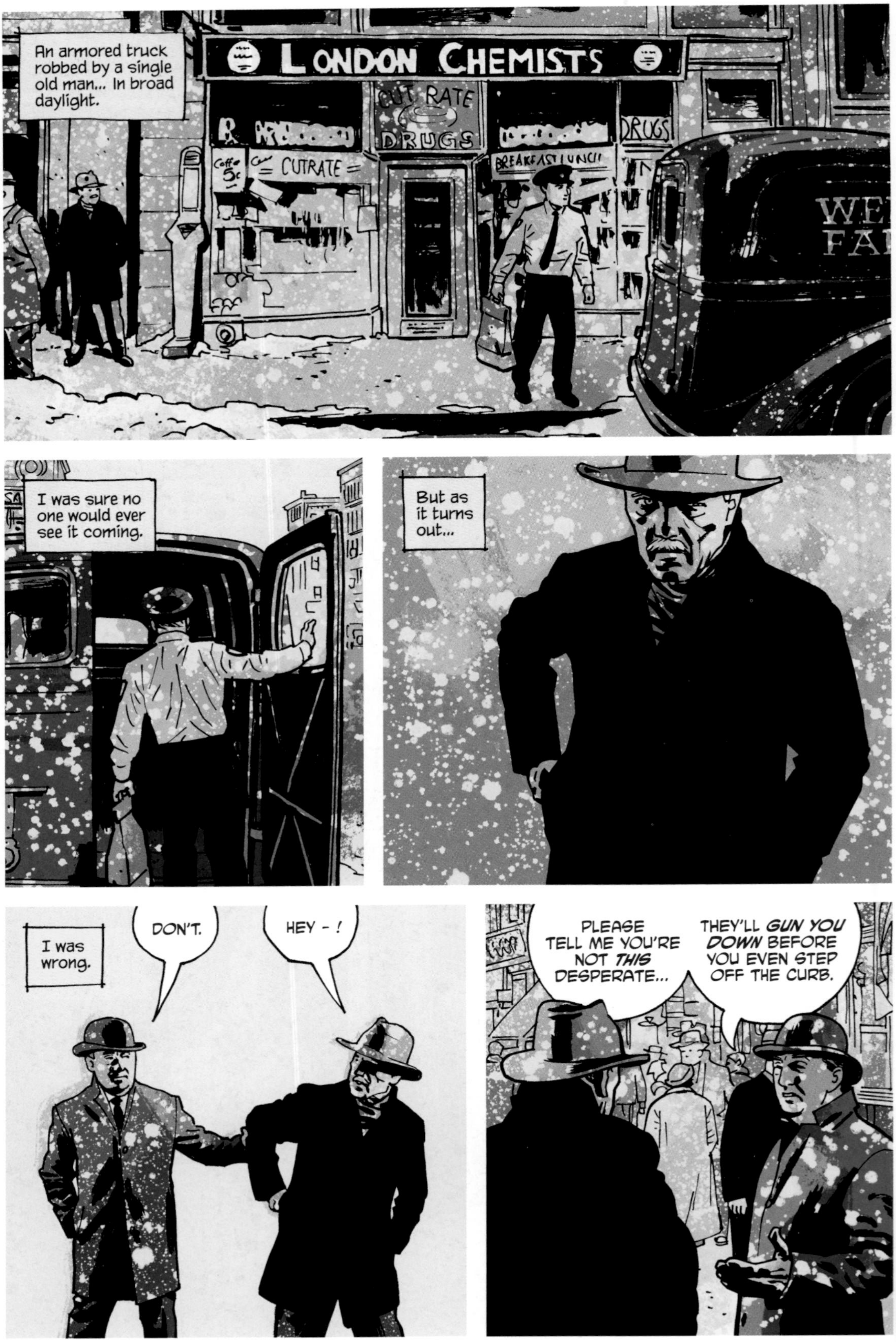
An armored truck robbed by a single old man... In broad daylight.
LONDON CHEMISTS
CUT RATE DRUGS
DRUGS
CUTRATE
BREAKFAST LUNCH
I was sure no one would ever see it coming.
But as it turns out...
I was wrong.
DON'T.
HEY - !
PLEASE TELL ME YOU'RE NOT THIS DESPERATE...
THEY'LL GUN YOU DOWN BEFORE YOU EVEN STEP OFF THE CURB.

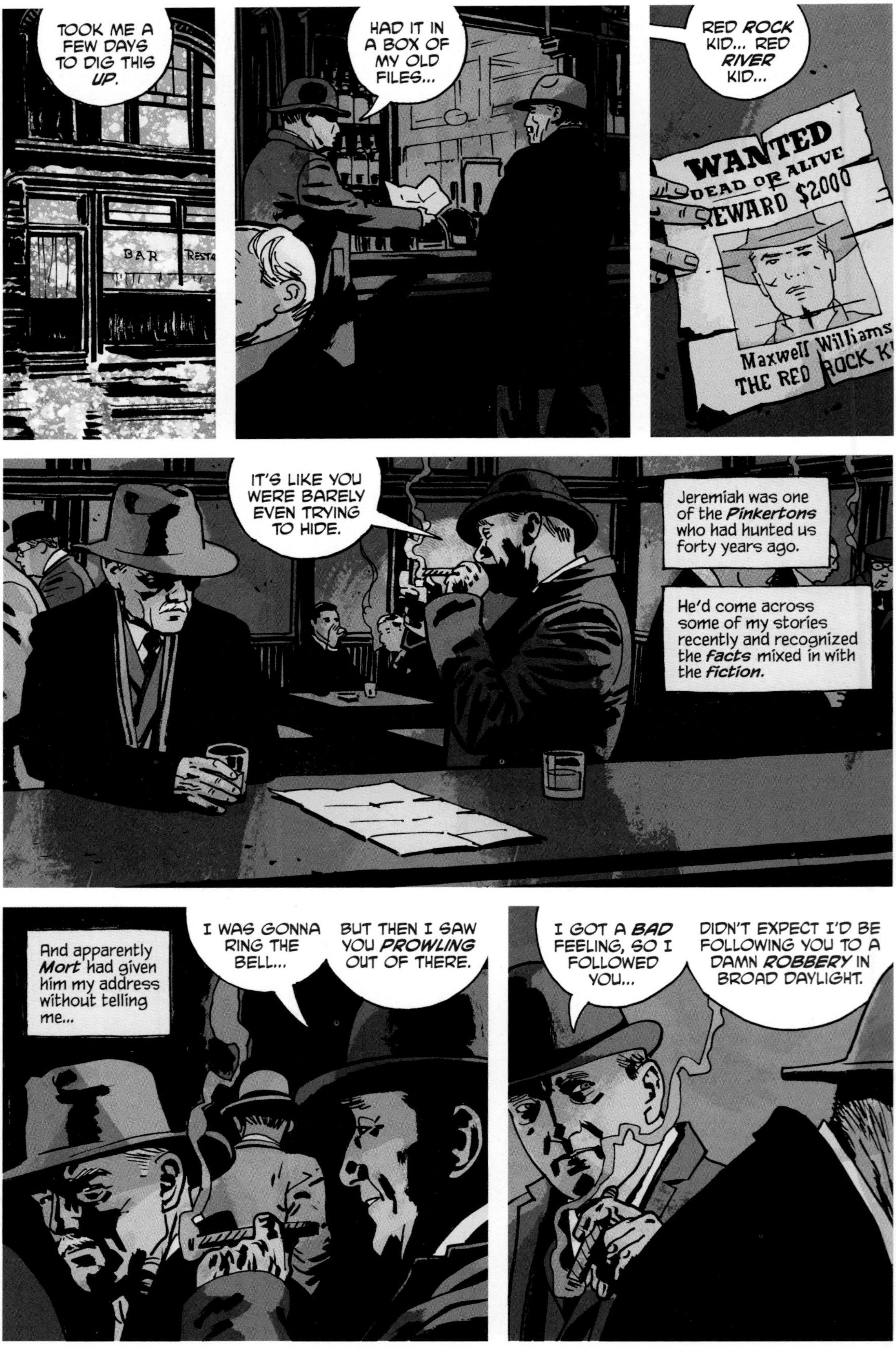

TOOK ME A FEW DAYS TO DIG THIS UP.
HAD IT IN A BOX OF MY OLD FILES...
RED ROCK KID... RED RIVER KID...
WANTED
DEAD OR ALIVE
REWARD $2000
Maxwell Williams
THE RED ROCK K
BAR
RESTA
IT'S LIKE YOU WERE BARELY EVEN TRYING TO HIDE.
Jeremiah was one of the Pinkertons who had hunted us forty years ago.
He'd come across some of my stories recently and recognized the facts mixed in with the fiction.
And apparently Mort had given him my address without telling me...
I WAS GONNA RING THE BELL...
BUT THEN I SAW YOU PROWLING OUT OF THERE.
I GOT A BAD FEELING, SO I FOLLOWED YOU...
DIDN'T EXPECT I'D BE FOLLOWING YOU TO A DAMN ROBBERY IN BROAD DAYLIGHT.

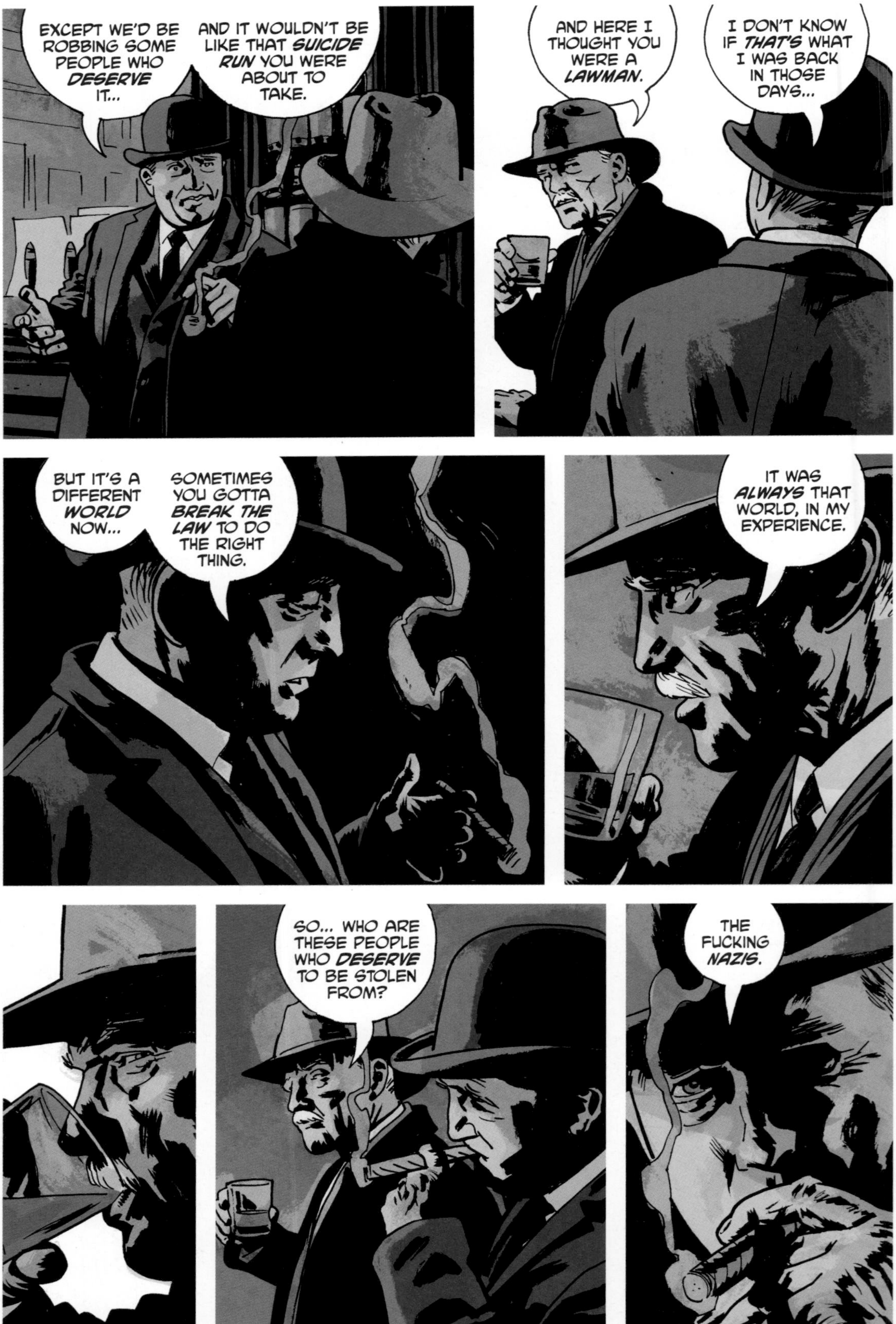
EXCEPT WE'D BE ROBBING SOME PEOPLE WHO DESERVE IT...
AND IT WOULDN'T BE LIKE THAT SUICIDE RUN YOU WERE ABOUT TO TAKE.
AND HERE I THOUGHT YOU WERE A LAWMAN.
I DON'T KNOW IF THAT'S WHAT I WAS BACK IN THOSE DAYS...
BUT IT'S A DIFFERENT WORLD NOW...
SOMETIMES YOU GOTTA BREAK THE LAW TO DO THE RIGHT THING.
IT WAS ALWAYS THAT WORLD, IN MY EXPERIENCE.
SO... WHO ARE THESE PEOPLE WHO DESERVE TO BE STOLEN FROM?
THE FUCKING NAZIS.

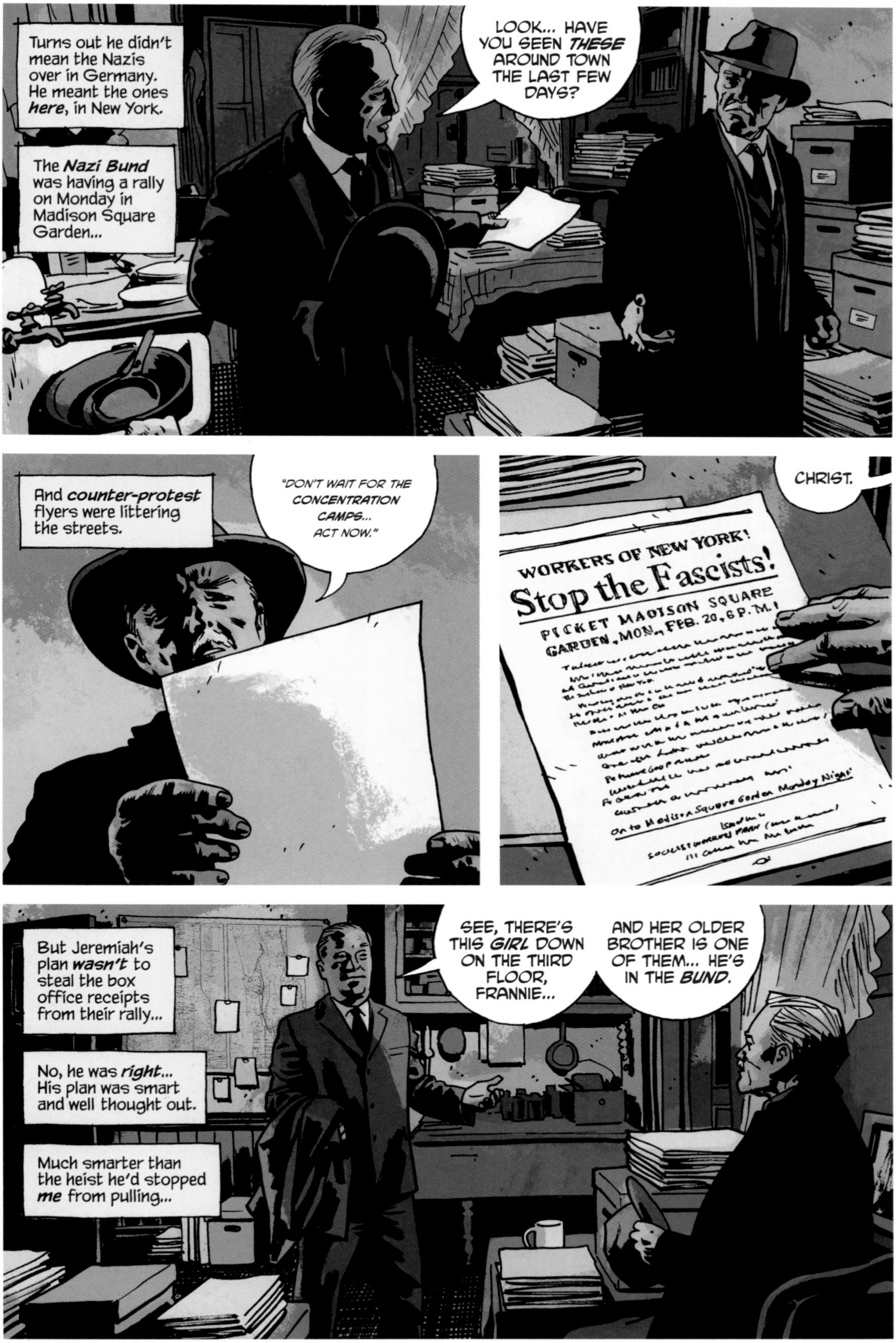

Turns out he didn't mean the Nazis over in Germany. He meant the ones *here*, in New York.
LOOK... HAVE YOU SEEN *THESE* AROUND TOWN THE LAST FEW DAYS?
The *Nazi Bund* was having a rally on Monday in Madison Square Garden...
And *counter-protest* flyers were littering the streets.
"DON'T WAIT FOR THE CONCENTRATION CAMPS... ACT NOW."
CHRIST.
WORKERS OF NEW YORK!
Stop the Fascists!
PICKET MADISON SQUARE GARDEN, MON., FEB. 20, 6 P.M.!
On to Madison Square Garden Monday Night
But Jeremiah's plan *wasn't* to steal the box office receipts from their rally...
SEE, THERE'S THIS *GIRL* DOWN ON THE THIRD FLOOR, FRANNIE...
AND HER OLDER BROTHER IS ONE OF THEM... HE'S IN THE *BUND*.
No, he was *right*... His plan was smart and well thought out.
Much smarter than the heist he'd stopped *me* from pulling...

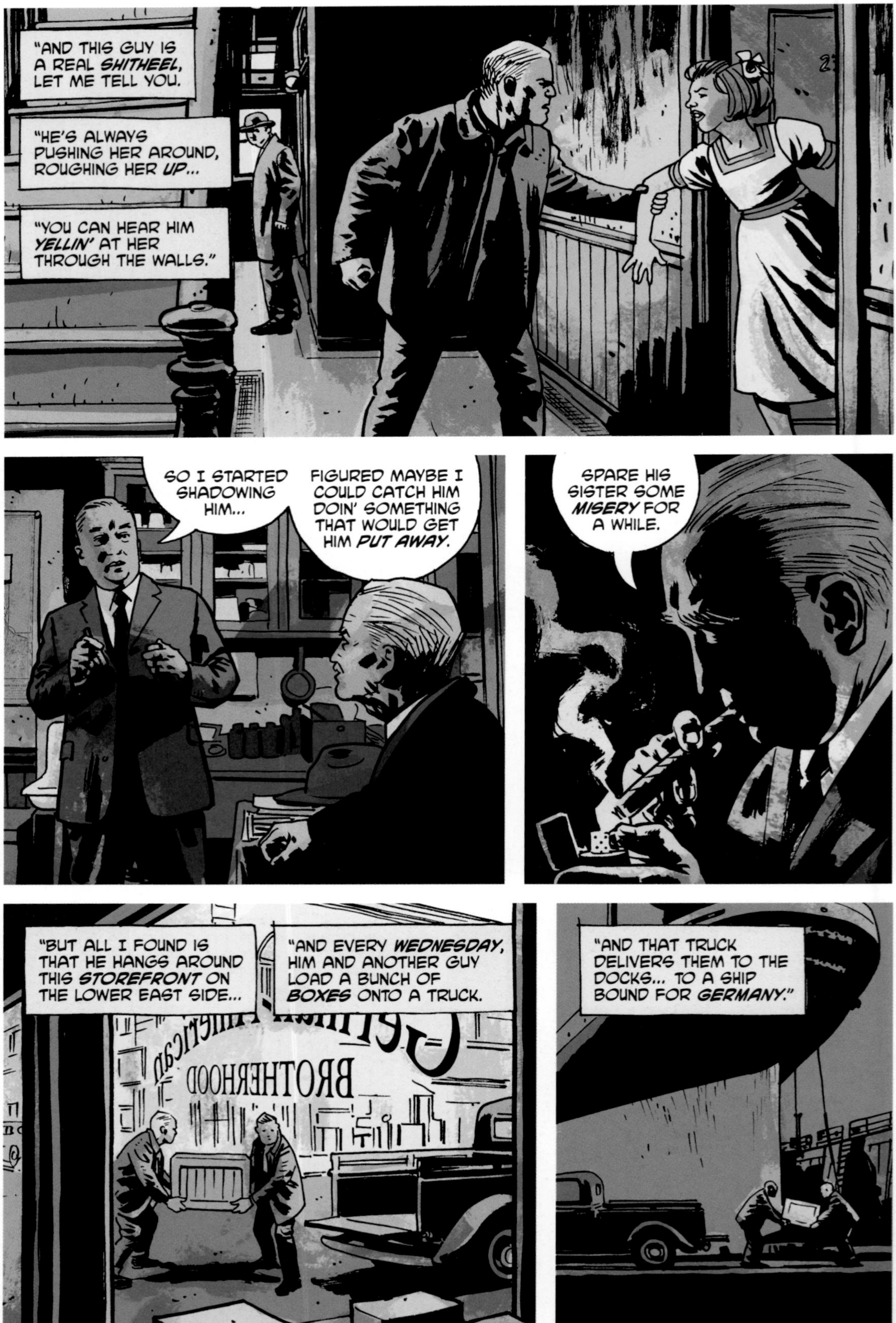

"AND THIS GUY IS A REAL *SHITHEEL*, LET ME TELL YOU.
"HE'S ALWAYS PUSHING HER AROUND, ROUGHING HER *UP*...
"YOU CAN HEAR HIM *YELLIN'* AT HER THROUGH THE WALLS."
SO I STARTED SHADOWING HIM...
FIGURED MAYBE I COULD CATCH HIM DOIN' SOMETHING THAT WOULD GET HIM *PUT AWAY*.
SPARE HIS SISTER SOME *MISERY* FOR A WHILE.
"BUT ALL I FOUND IS THAT HE HANGS AROUND THIS *STOREFRONT* ON THE LOWER EAST SIDE...
"AND EVERY *WEDNESDAY*, HIM AND ANOTHER GUY LOAD A BUNCH OF *BOXES* ONTO A TRUCK.
BROTHERHOOD
"AND THAT TRUCK DELIVERS THEM TO THE DOCKS... TO A SHIP BOUND FOR *GERMANY*."

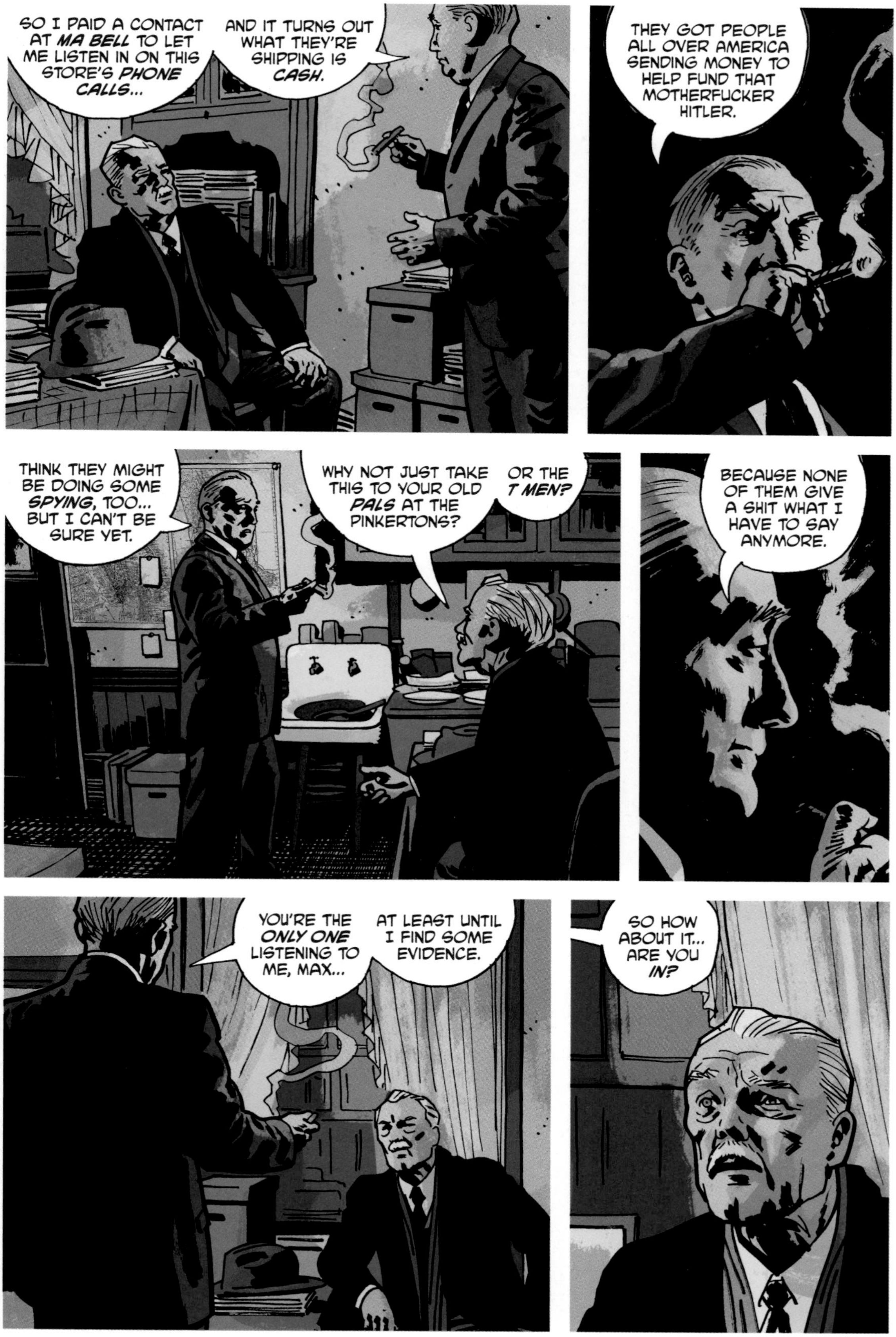
SO I PAID A CONTACT AT MA BELL TO LET ME LISTEN IN ON THIS STORE'S PHONE CALLS...
AND IT TURNS OUT WHAT THEY'RE SHIPPING IS CASH.
THEY GOT PEOPLE ALL OVER AMERICA SENDING MONEY TO HELP FUND THAT MOTHERFUCKER HITLER.
THINK THEY MIGHT BE DOING SOME SPYING, TOO... BUT I CAN'T BE SURE YET.
WHY NOT JUST TAKE THIS TO YOUR OLD PALS AT THE PINKERTONS?
OR THE T MEN?
BECAUSE NONE OF THEM GIVE A SHIT WHAT I HAVE TO SAY ANYMORE.
YOU'RE THE ONLY ONE LISTENING TO ME, MAX...
AT LEAST UNTIL I FIND SOME EVIDENCE.
SO HOW ABOUT IT... ARE YOU IN?

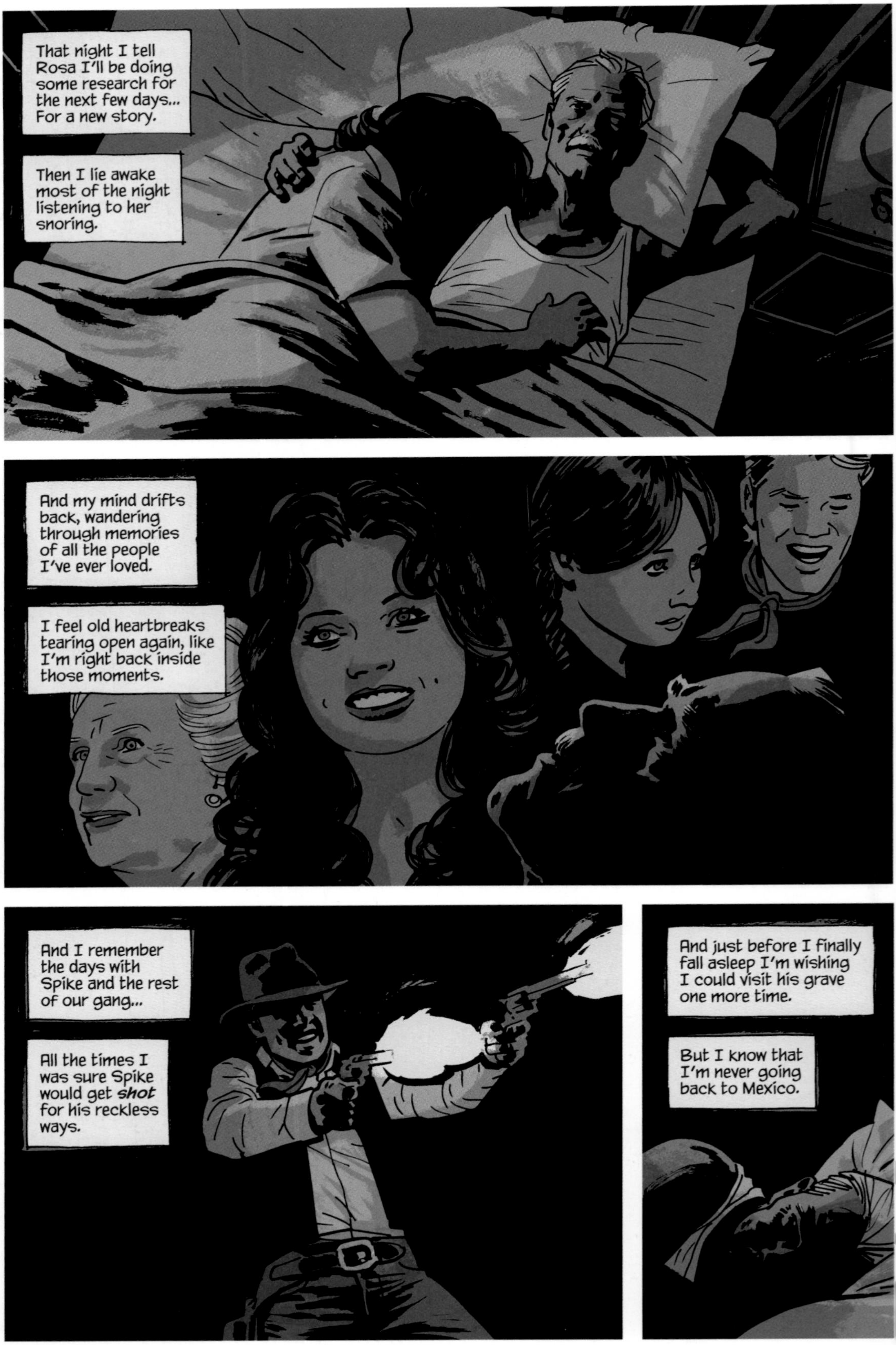
That night I tell Rosa I'll be doing some research for the next few days... For a new story.
Then I lie awake most of the night listening to her snoring.
And my mind drifts back, wandering through memories of all the people I've ever loved.
I feel old heartbreaks tearing open again, like I'm right back inside those moments.
And I remember the days with Spike and the rest of our gang...
All the times I was sure Spike would get *shot* for his reckless ways.
And just before I finally fall asleep I'm wishing I could visit his grave one more time.
But I know that I'm never going back to Mexico.

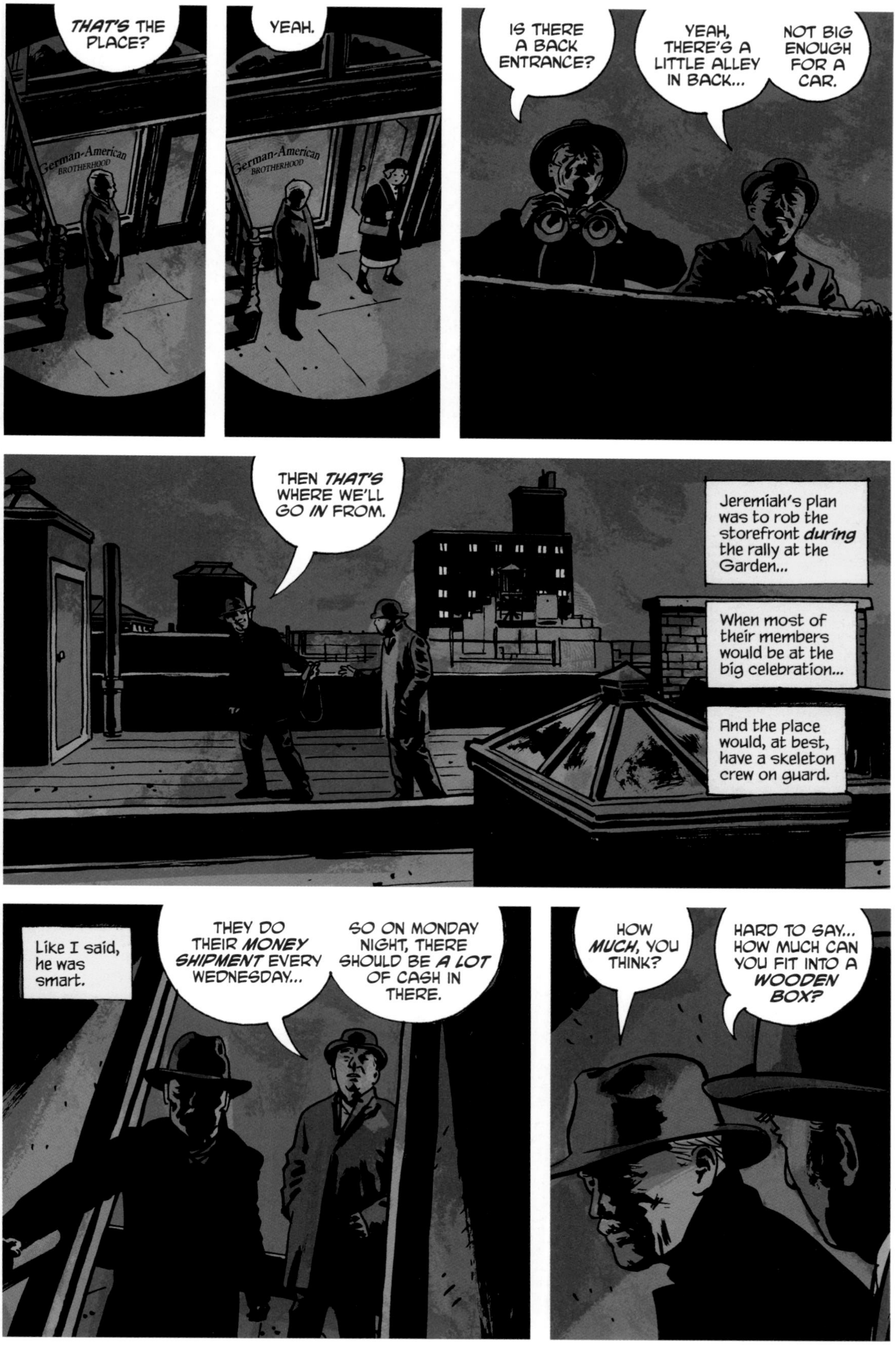
THAT'S THE PLACE?
German-American BROTHERHOOD
YEAH.
German-American BROTHERHOOD
IS THERE A BACK ENTRANCE?
YEAH, THERE'S A LITTLE ALLEY IN BACK...
NOT BIG ENOUGH FOR A CAR.
THEN THAT'S WHERE WE'LL GO IN FROM.
Jeremiah's plan was to rob the storefront during the rally at the Garden...
When most of their members would be at the big celebration...
And the place would, at best, have a skeleton crew on guard.
Like I said, he was smart.
THEY DO THEIR MONEY SHIPMENT EVERY WEDNESDAY...
SO ON MONDAY NIGHT, THERE SHOULD BE A LOT OF CASH IN THERE.
HOW MUCH, YOU THINK?
HARD TO SAY... HOW MUCH CAN YOU FIT INTO A WOODEN BOX?

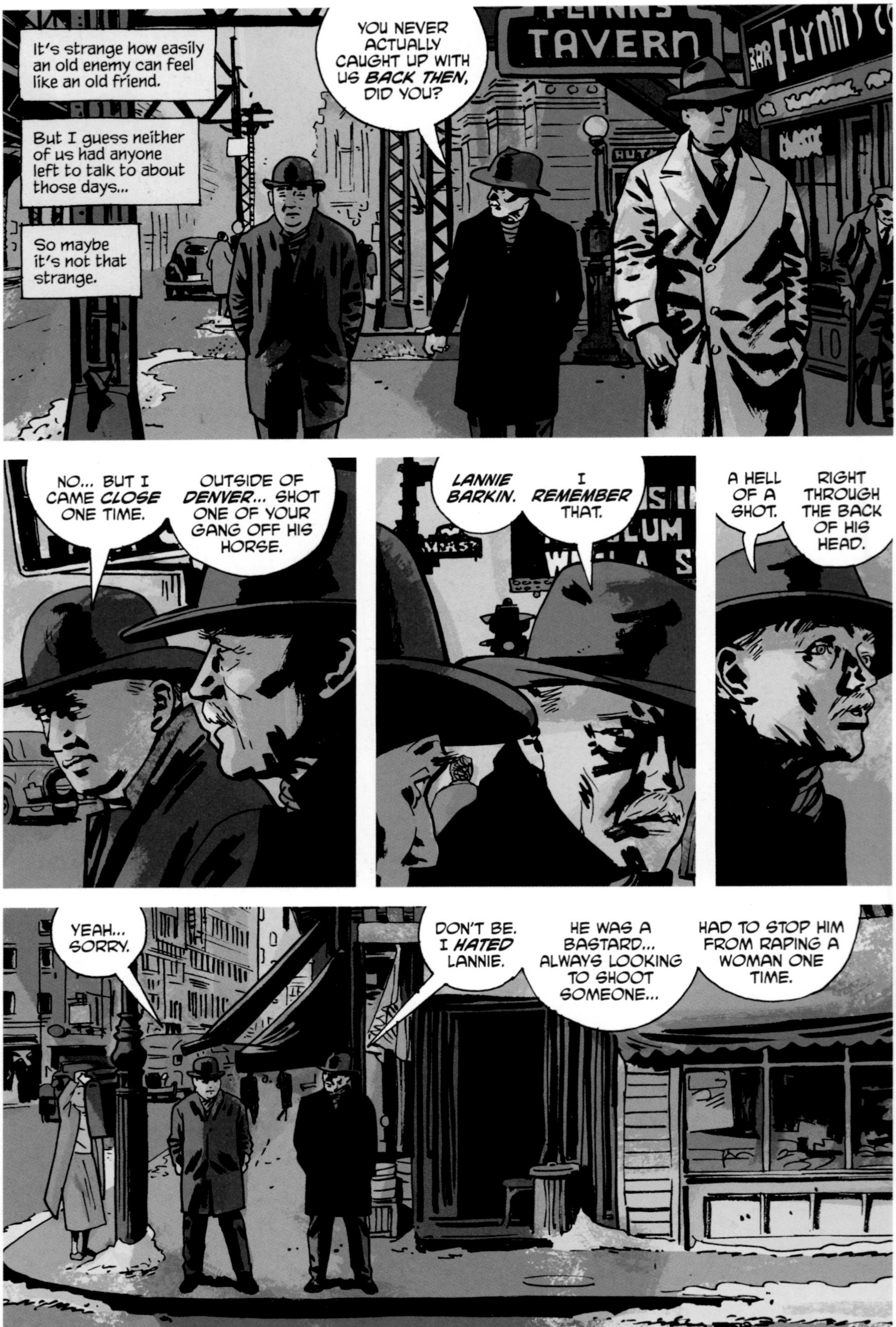

It's strange how easily an old enemy can feel like an old friend.
But I guess neither of us had anyone left to talk to about those days...
So maybe it's not that strange.
YOU NEVER ACTUALLY CAUGHT UP WITH US *BACK THEN*, DID YOU?
FLYNN'S TAVERN
FLYNN'S
NO... BUT I CAME *CLOSE* ONE TIME.
OUTSIDE OF *DENVER*... SHOT ONE OF YOUR GANG OFF HIS HORSE.
LANNIE BARKIN.
I *REMEMBER* THAT.
A HELL OF A SHOT.
RIGHT THROUGH THE BACK OF HIS HEAD.
YEAH... SORRY.
DON'T BE. I *HATED* LANNIE.
HE WAS A BASTARD... ALWAYS LOOKING TO SHOOT SOMEONE...
HAD TO STOP HIM FROM RAPING A WOMAN ONE TIME.

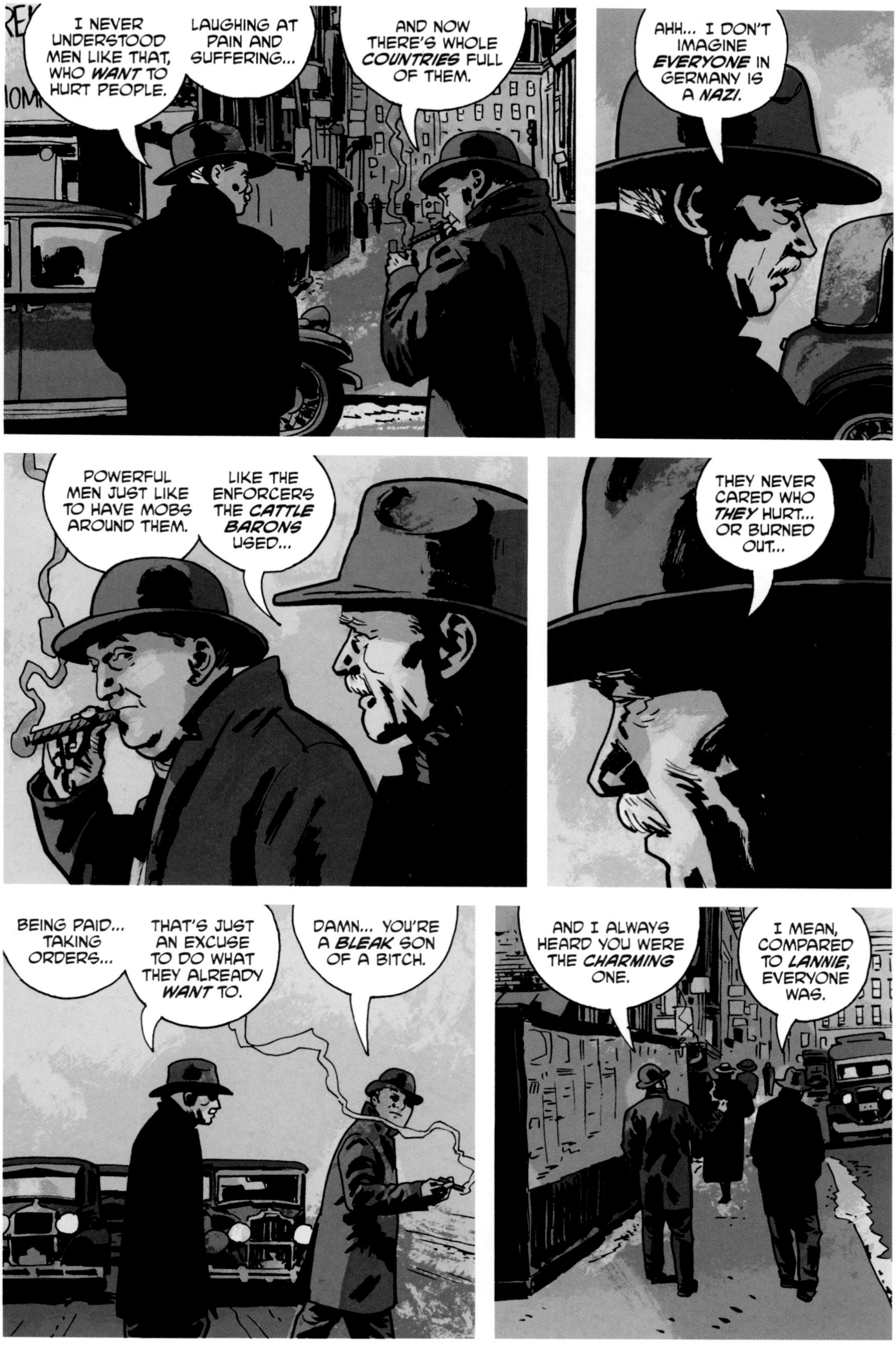
I NEVER UNDERSTOOD MEN LIKE THAT, WHO *WANT* TO HURT PEOPLE.
LAUGHING AT PAIN AND SUFFERING...
AND NOW THERE'S WHOLE *COUNTRIES* FULL OF THEM.
AHH... I DON'T IMAGINE *EVERYONE* IN GERMANY IS A *NAZI*.
POWERFUL MEN JUST LIKE TO HAVE MOBS AROUND THEM.
LIKE THE ENFORCERS THE *CATTLE BARONS* USED...
THEY NEVER CARED WHO *THEY* HURT... OR BURNED OUT...
BEING PAID... TAKING ORDERS...
THAT'S JUST AN EXCUSE TO DO WHAT THEY ALREADY *WANT* TO.
DAMN... YOU'RE A *BLEAK* SON OF A BITCH.
AND I ALWAYS HEARD YOU WERE THE *CHARMING* ONE.
I MEAN, COMPARED TO *LANNIE*, EVERYONE WAS.

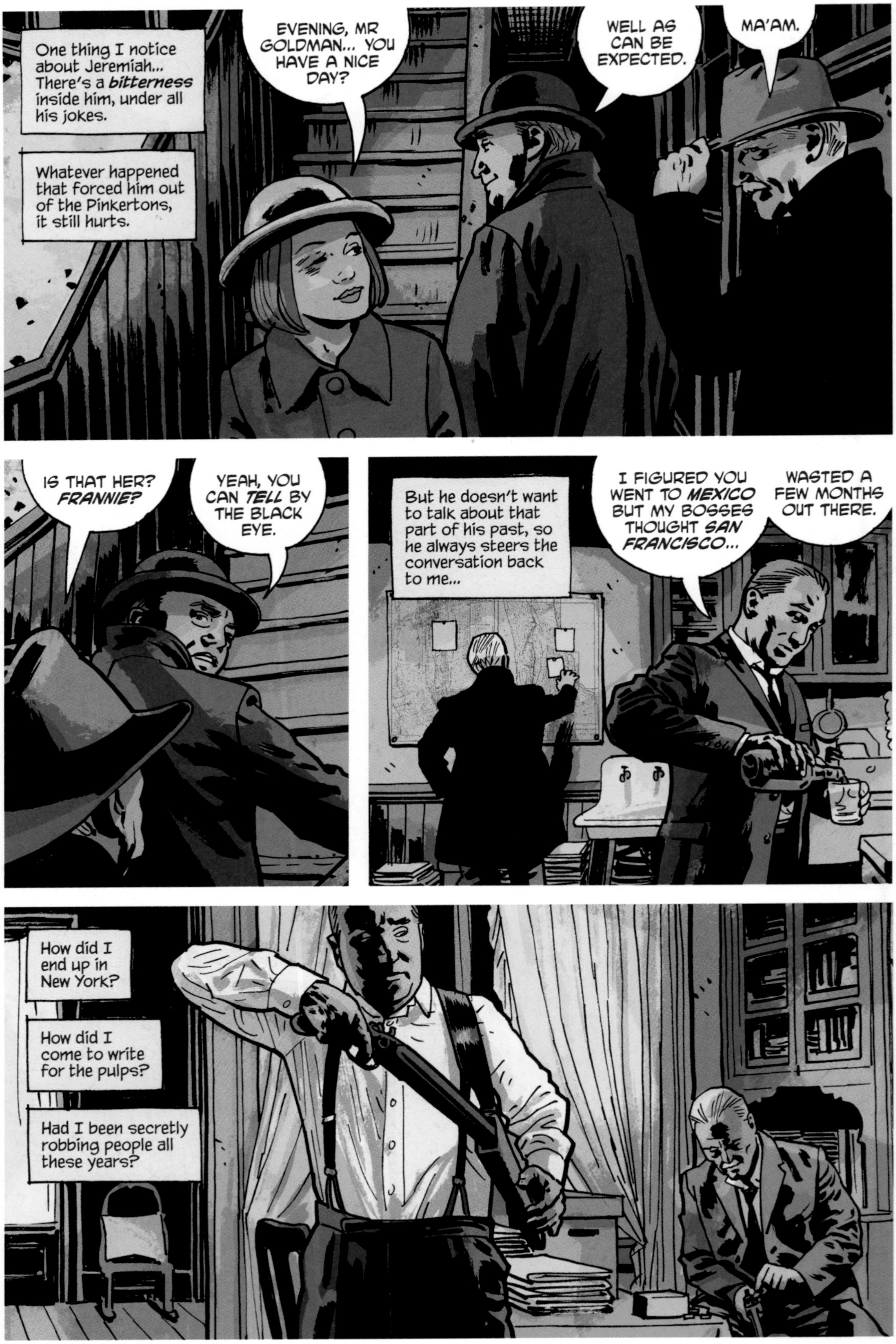
One thing I notice about Jeremiah... There's a *bitterness* inside him, under all his jokes.
Whatever happened that forced him out of the Pinkertons, it still hurts.
EVENING, MR GOLDMAN... YOU HAVE A NICE DAY?
WELL AS CAN BE EXPECTED.
MA'AM.
IS THAT HER? *FRANNIE?*
YEAH, YOU CAN *TELL* BY THE BLACK EYE.
But he doesn't want to talk about that part of his past, so he always steers the conversation back to me...
I FIGURED YOU WENT TO *MEXICO* BUT MY BOSSES THOUGHT *SAN FRANCISCO*...
WASTED A FEW MONTHS OUT THERE.
How did I end up in New York?
How did I come to write for the pulps?
Had I been secretly robbing people all these years?

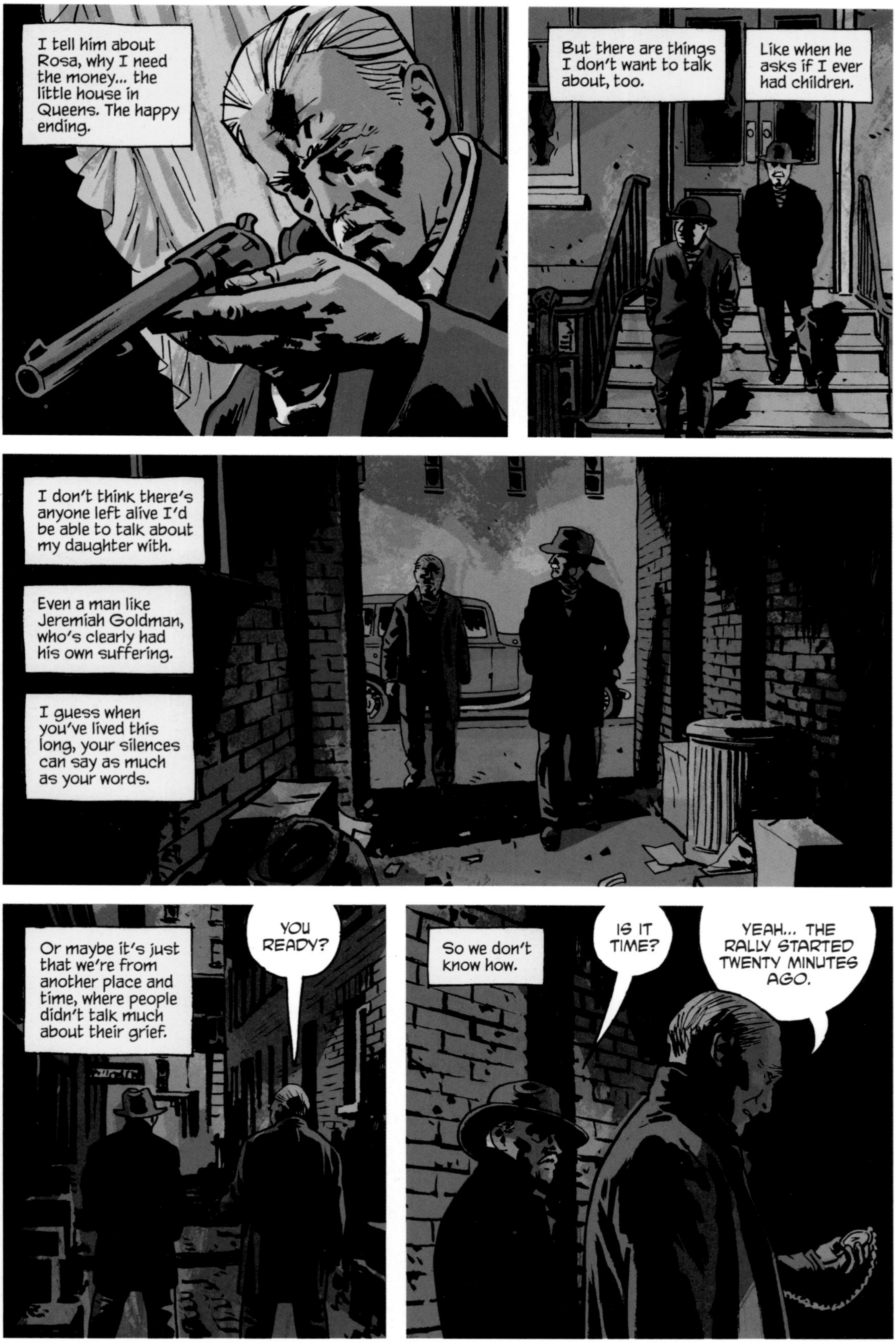

I tell him about Rosa, why I need the money... the little house in Queens. The happy ending.
But there are things I don't want to talk about, too.
Like when he asks if I ever had children.
I don't think there's anyone left alive I'd be able to talk about my daughter with.
Even a man like Jeremiah Goldman, who's clearly had his own suffering.
I guess when you've lived this long, your silences can say as much as your words.
Or maybe it's just that we're from another place and time, where people didn't talk much about their grief.
YOU READY?
So we don't know how.
IS IT TIME?
YEAH... THE RALLY STARTED TWENTY MINUTES AGO.

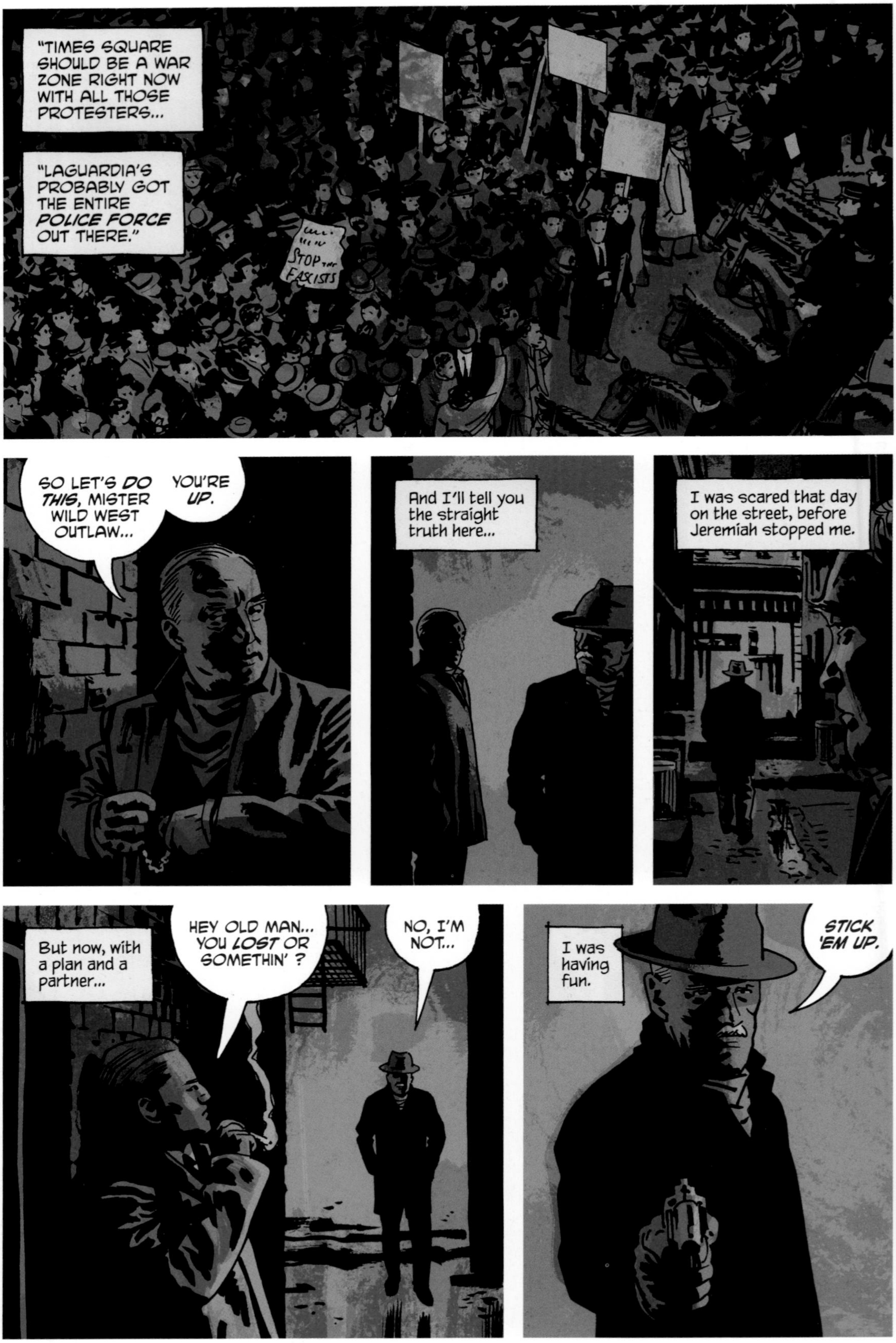
"TIMES SQUARE SHOULD BE A WAR ZONE RIGHT NOW WITH ALL THOSE PROTESTERS...
"LAGUARDIA'S PROBABLY GOT THE ENTIRE POLICE FORCE OUT THERE."
STOP THE FASCISTS
SO LET'S DO THIS, MISTER WILD WEST OUTLAW...
YOU'RE UP.
And I'll tell you the straight truth here...
I was scared that day on the street, before Jeremiah stopped me.
But now, with a plan and a partner...
HEY OLD MAN... YOU LOST OR SOMETHIN' ?
NO, I'M NOT...
I was having fun.
STICK 'EM UP.

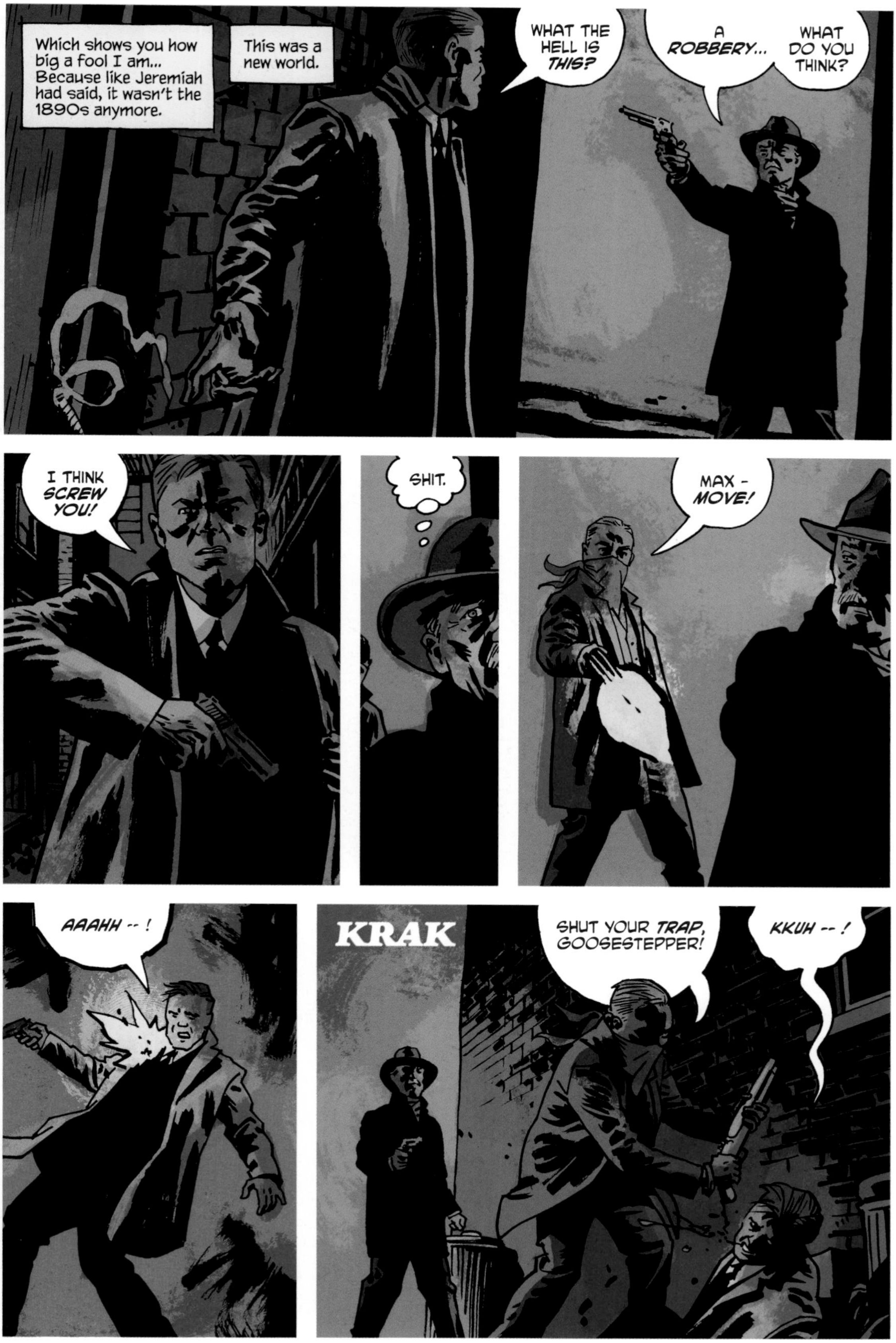
Which shows you how big a fool I am... Because like Jeremiah had said, it wasn't the 1890s anymore.
This was a new world.
WHAT THE HELL IS THIS?
A ROBBERY...
WHAT DO YOU THINK?
I THINK SCREW YOU!
SHIT.
MAX - MOVE!
AAAHH -- !
KRAK
SHUT YOUR TRAP, GOOSESTEPPER!
KKUH -- !

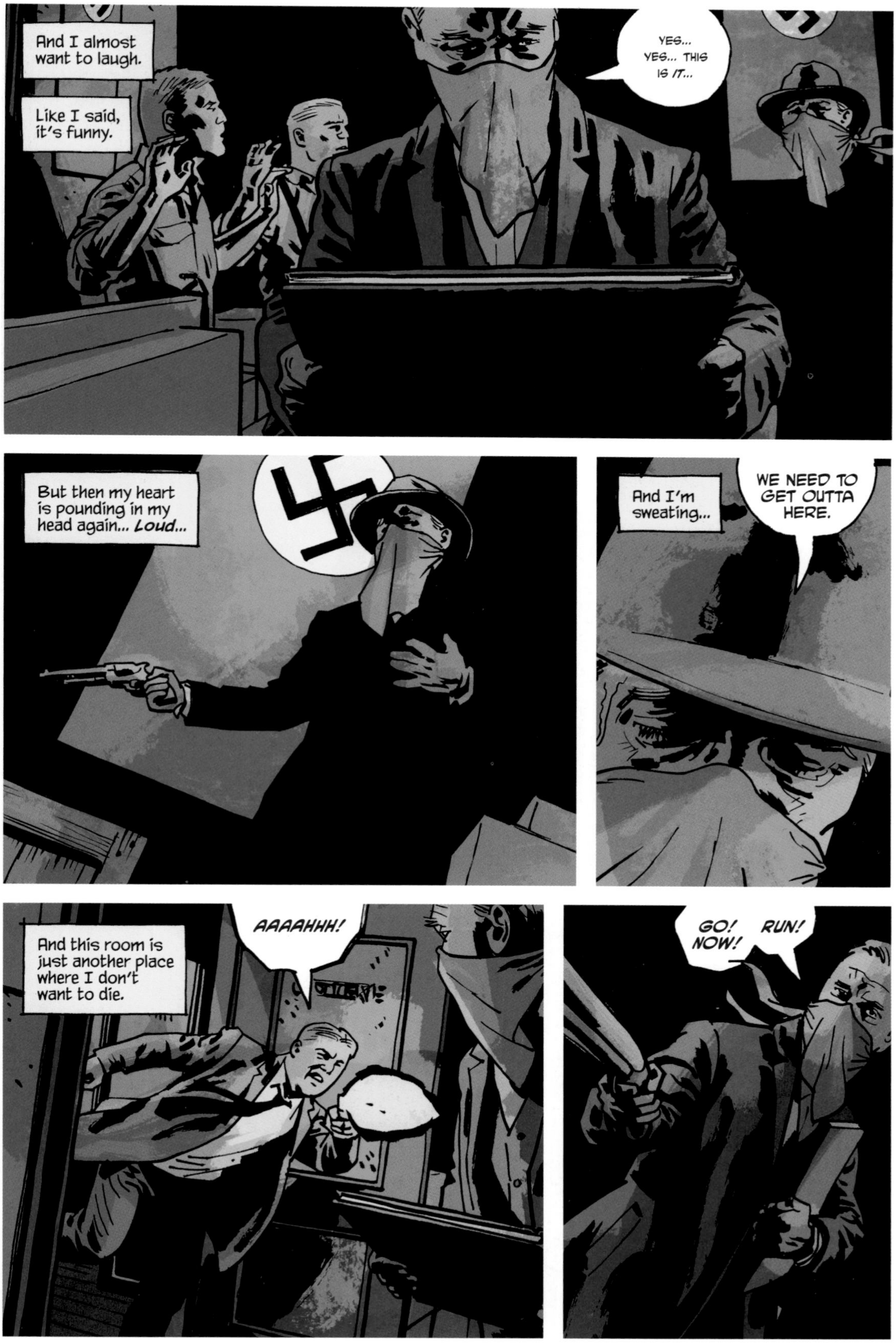
And I almost want to laugh.
Like I said, it's funny.
YES... YES... THIS IS *IT*...
But then my heart is pounding in my head again... *Loud*...
And I'm sweating...
WE NEED TO GET OUTTA HERE.
And this room is just another place where I don't want to die.
AAAAHHH!
GO! NOW!
RUN!

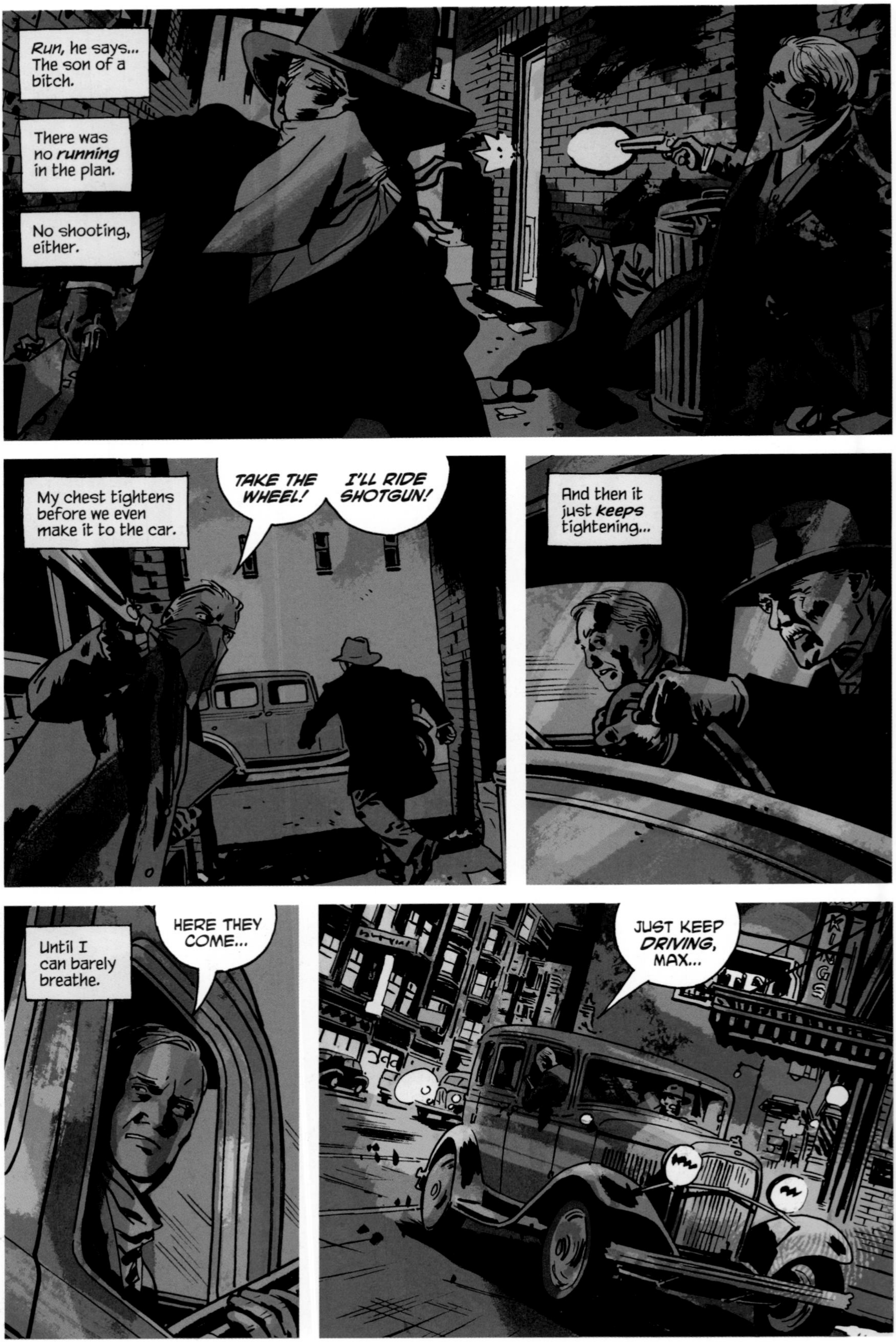
Run, he says... The son of a bitch.
There was no running in the plan.
No shooting, either.
My chest tightens before we even make it to the car.
TAKE THE WHEEL!
I'LL RIDE SHOTGUN!
And then it just keeps tightening...
Until I can barely breathe.
HERE THEY COME...
JUST KEEP DRIVING, MAX...

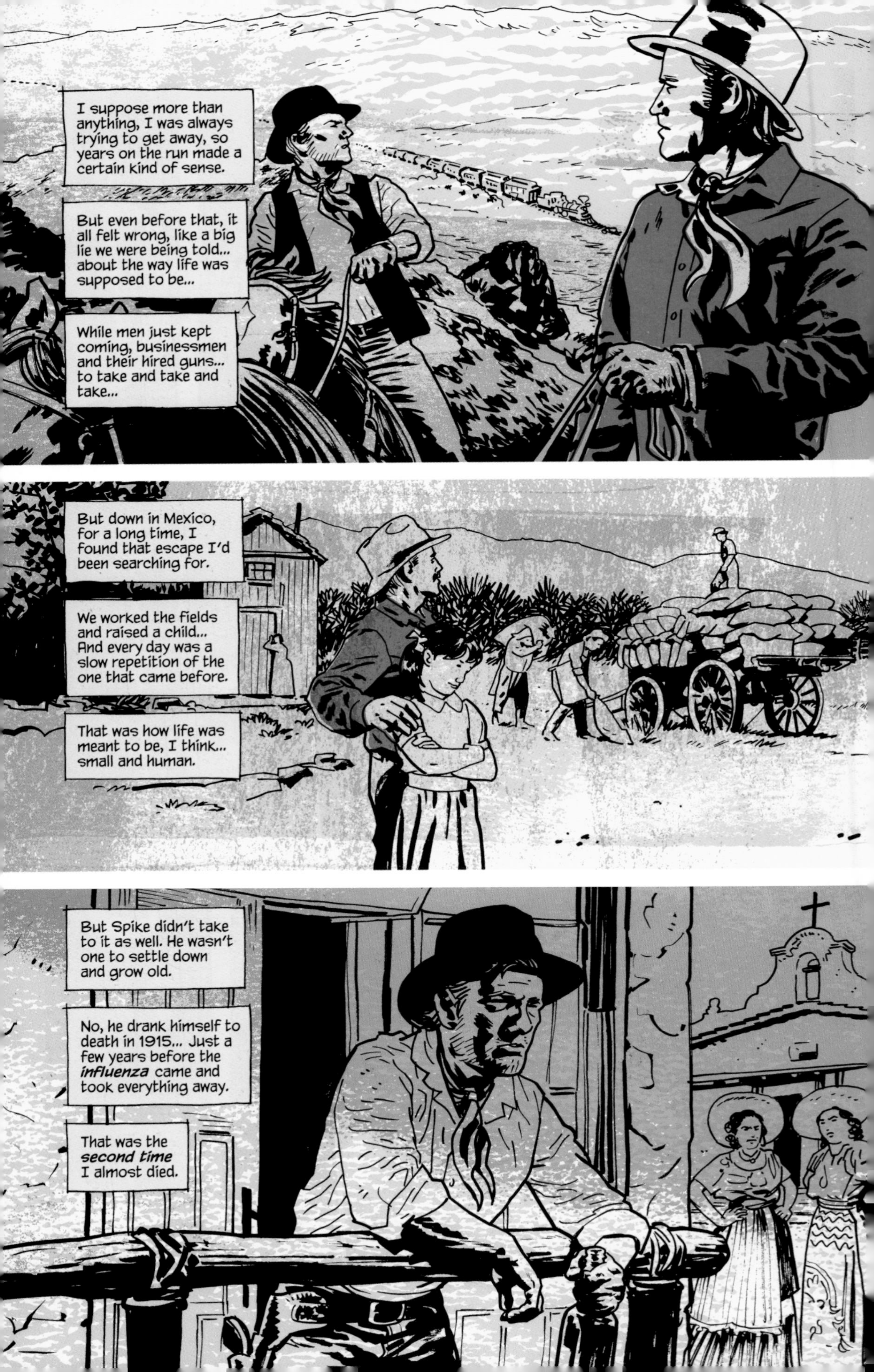
I suppose more than anything, I was always trying to get away, so years on the run made a certain kind of sense.
But even before that, it all felt wrong, like a big lie we were being told... about the way life was supposed to be...
While men just kept coming, businessmen and their hired guns... to take and take and take...
But down in Mexico, for a long time, I found that escape I'd been searching for.
We worked the fields and raised a child... And every day was a slow repetition of the one that came before.
That was how life was meant to be, I think... small and human.
But Spike didn't take to it as well. He wasn't one to settle down and grow old.
No, he drank himself to death in 1915... Just a few years before the *influenza* came and took everything away.
That was the *second time* I almost died.

YOU... MAX? AWAKE...?

...WHUU...?

HEY... DID YOU KNOW YOU'VE GOT A *HEART CONDITION?*

YOU... SON OF A BITCH...

WAS THERE *EVER* ANY *MONEY...?*

YEAH, THERE'S MONEY... JUST NOT IN THAT OFFICE...

IT GETS TRANSFERRED BY THE INTERNATIONAL *BANKS.*

BUT THAT OFFICE IS WHERE THE *ACCOUNTING* IS DONE.

RECORDS OF WHO *DONATED* AND HOW MUCH...

YOU WOULDN'T BELIEVE HOW MANY *IMPORTANT* AMERICANS ARE *SECRETLY* NAZIS, MAX.

THAT'S WHAT YOU WERE AFTER THE WHOLE TIME?

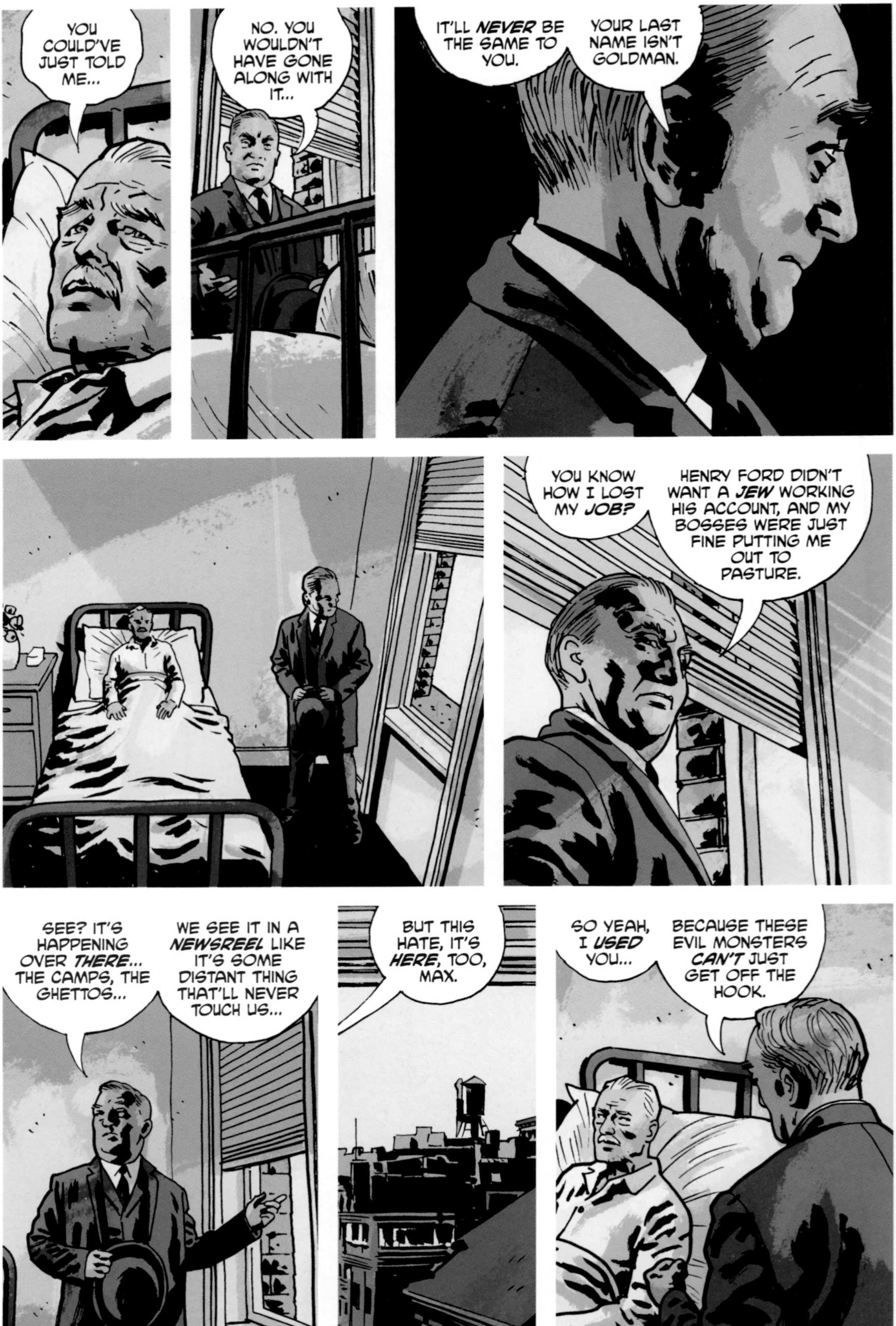
YOU COULD'VE JUST TOLD ME...
NO. YOU WOULDN'T HAVE GONE ALONG WITH IT...
IT'LL NEVER BE THE SAME TO YOU.
YOUR LAST NAME ISN'T GOLDMAN.
YOU KNOW HOW I LOST MY JOB?
HENRY FORD DIDN'T WANT A JEW WORKING HIS ACCOUNT, AND MY BOSSES WERE JUST FINE PUTTING ME OUT TO PASTURE.
SEE? IT'S HAPPENING OVER THERE... THE CAMPS, THE GHETTOS...
WE SEE IT IN A NEWSREEL LIKE IT'S SOME DISTANT THING THAT'LL NEVER TOUCH US...
BUT THIS HATE, IT'S HERE, TOO, MAX.
SO YEAH, I USED YOU...
BECAUSE THESE EVIL MONSTERS CAN'T JUST GET OFF THE HOOK.

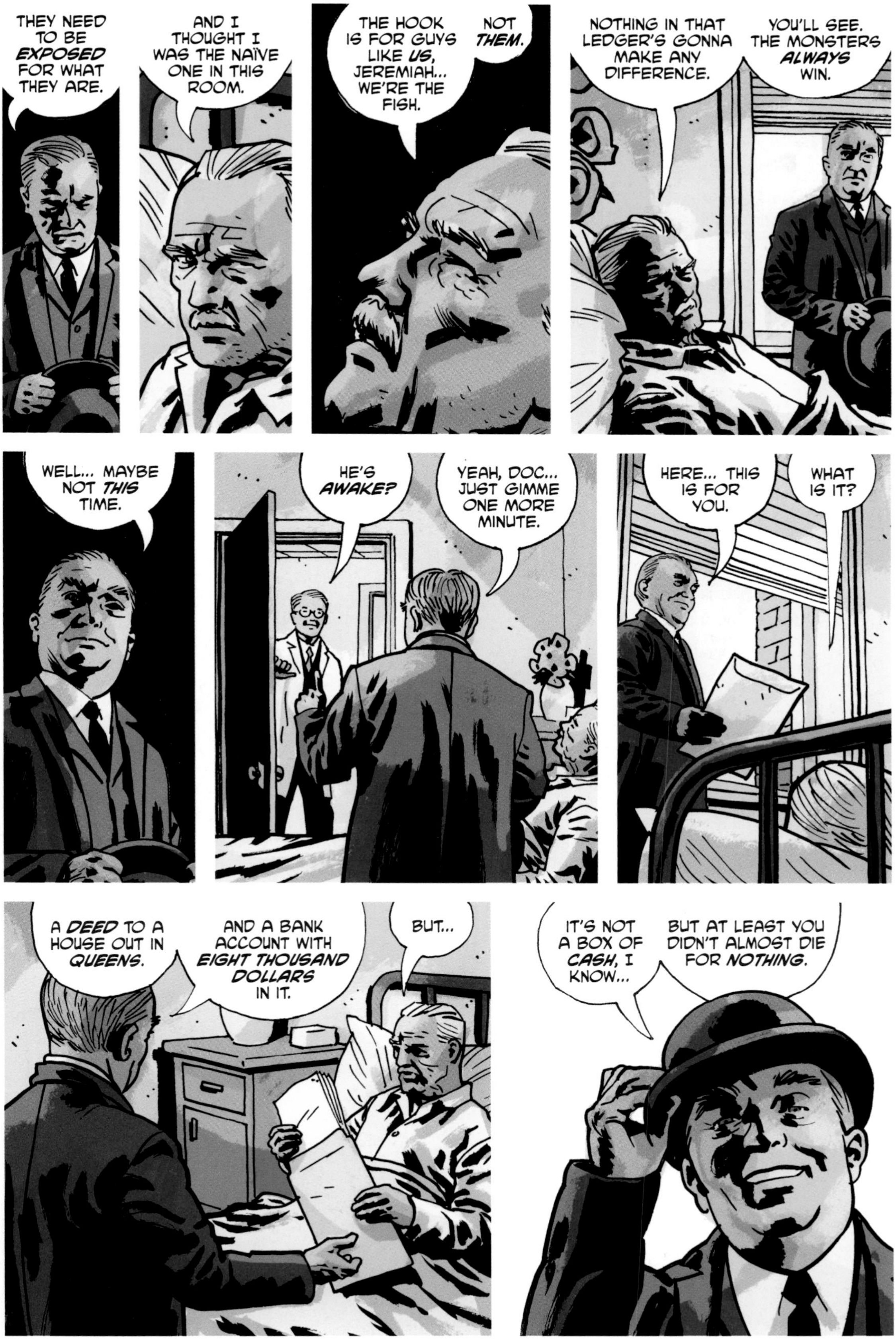
THEY NEED TO BE EXPOSED FOR WHAT THEY ARE.
AND I THOUGHT I WAS THE NAÏVE ONE IN THIS ROOM.
THE HOOK IS FOR GUYS LIKE US, JEREMIAH... WE'RE THE FISH.
NOT THEM.
NOTHING IN THAT LEDGER'S GONNA MAKE ANY DIFFERENCE.
YOU'LL SEE. THE MONSTERS ALWAYS WIN.
WELL... MAYBE NOT THIS TIME.
HE'S AWAKE?
YEAH, DOC... JUST GIMME ONE MORE MINUTE.
HERE... THIS IS FOR YOU.
WHAT IS IT?
A DEED TO A HOUSE OUT IN QUEENS.
AND A BANK ACCOUNT WITH EIGHT THOUSAND DOLLARS IN IT.
BUT...
IT'S NOT A BOX OF CASH, I KNOW...
BUT AT LEAST YOU DIDN'T ALMOST DIE FOR NOTHING.

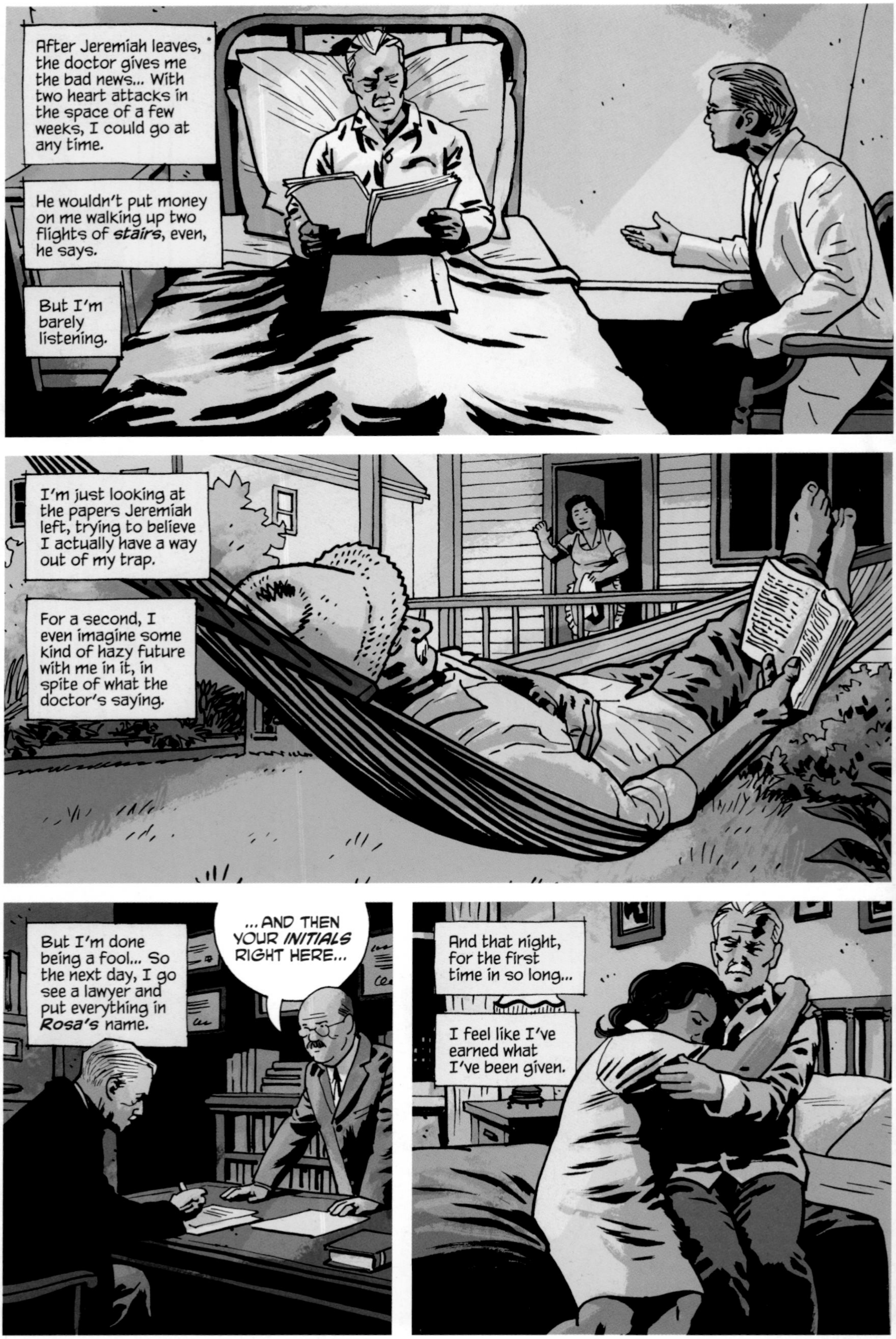
After Jeremiah leaves, the doctor gives me the bad news... With two heart attacks in the space of a few weeks, I could go at any time.
He wouldn't put money on me walking up two flights of *stairs*, even, he says.
But I'm barely listening.
I'm just looking at the papers Jeremiah left, trying to believe I actually have a way out of my trap.
For a second, I even imagine some kind of hazy future with me in it, in spite of what the doctor's saying.
But I'm done being a fool... So the next day, I go see a lawyer and put everything in *Rosa's* name.
...AND THEN YOUR *INITIALS* RIGHT HERE...
And that night, for the first time in so long...
I feel like I've earned what I've been given.

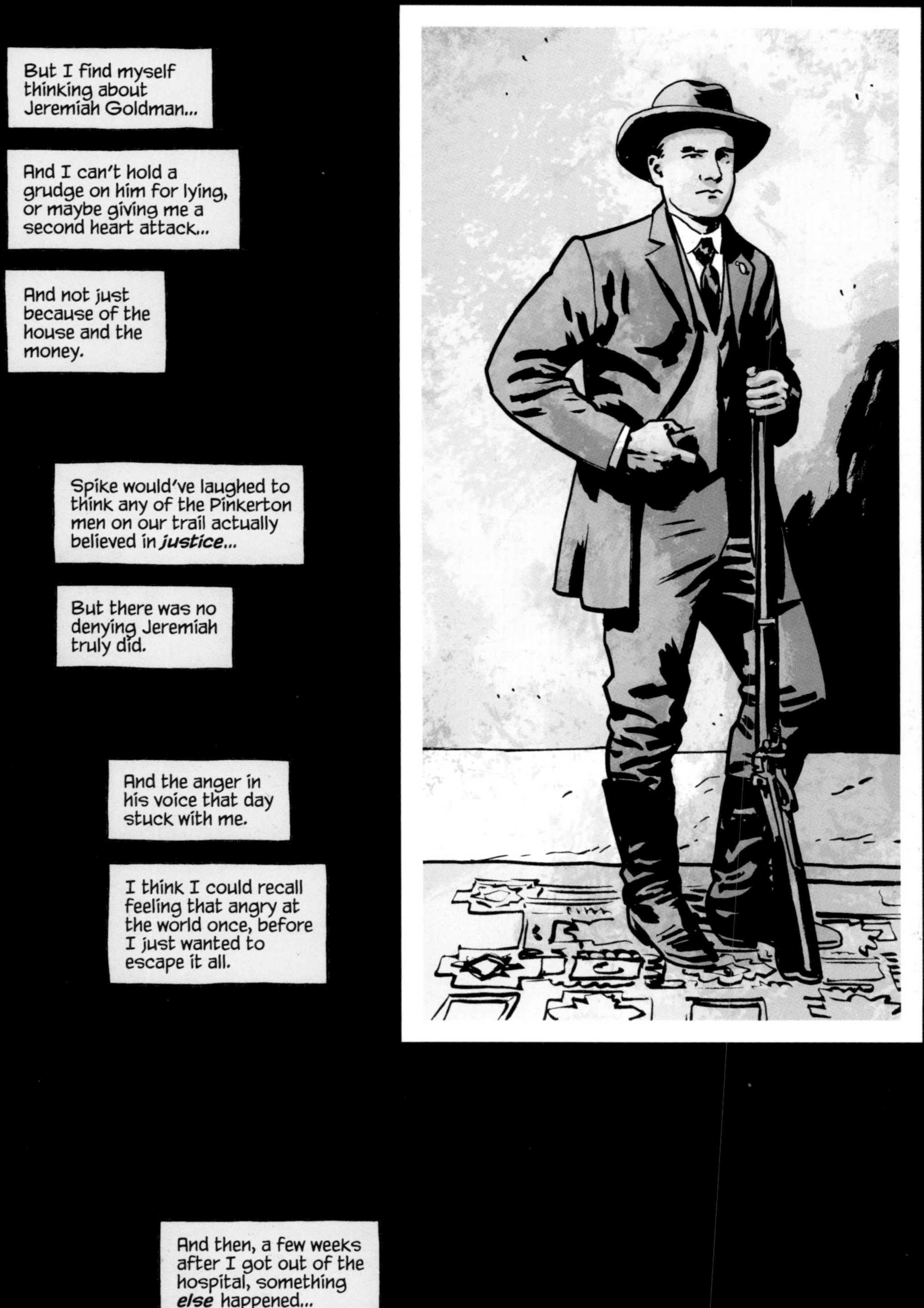
But I find myself thinking about Jeremiah Goldman...
And I can't hold a grudge on him for lying, or maybe giving me a second heart attack...
And not just because of the house and the money.
Spike would've laughed to think any of the Pinkerton men on our trail actually believed in *justice*...
But there was no denying Jeremiah truly did.
And the anger in his voice that day stuck with me.
I think I could recall feeling that angry at the world once, before I just wanted to escape it all.
And then, a few weeks after I got out of the hospital, something *else* happened...

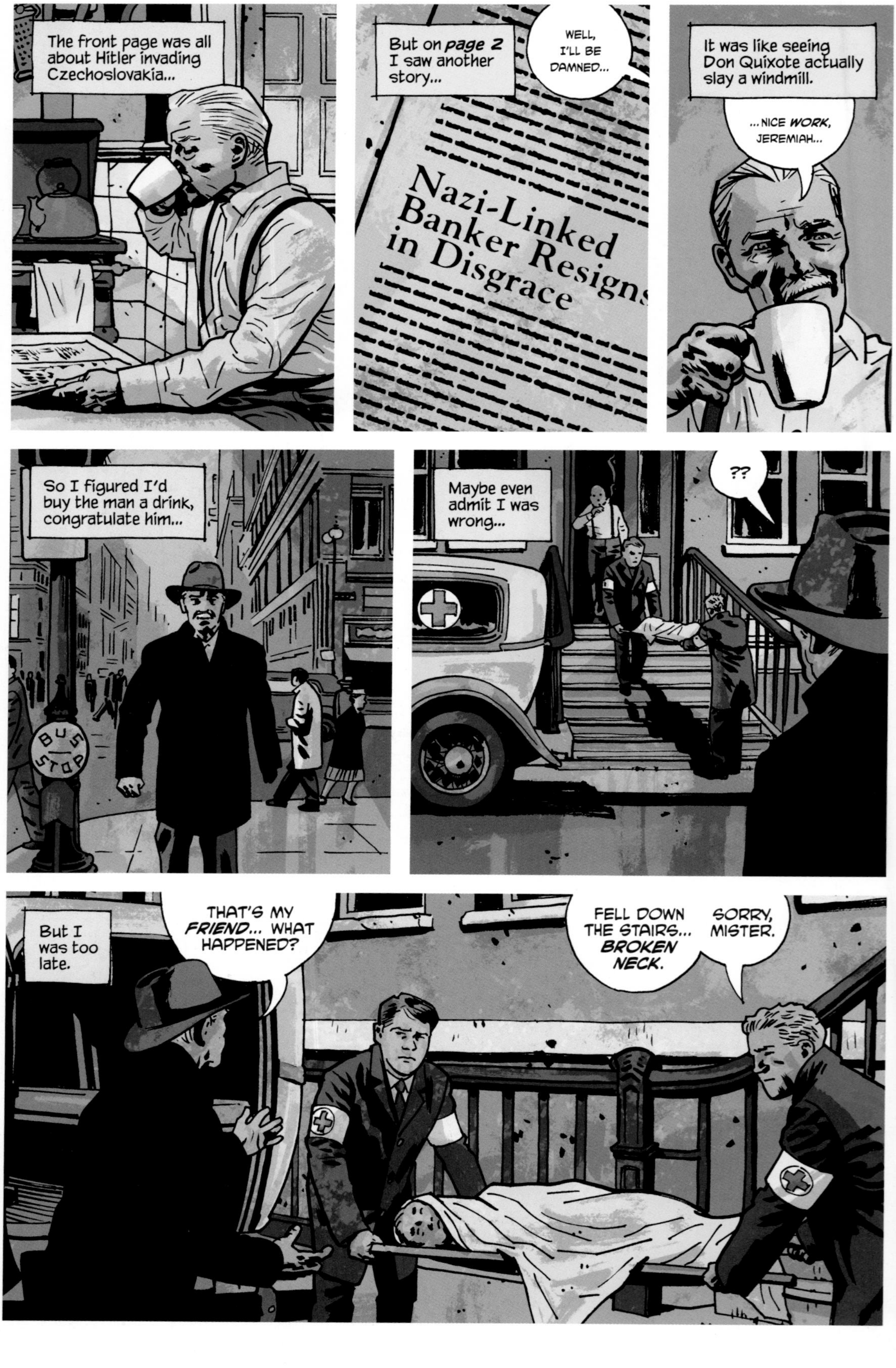
The front page was all about Hitler invading Czechoslovakia...
But on *page 2* I saw another story...
WELL, I'LL BE DAMNED...
Nazi-Linked Banker Resigns in Disgrace
It was like seeing Don Quixote actually slay a windmill.
...NICE *WORK*, JEREMIAH...
So I figured I'd buy the man a drink, congratulate him...
BUS STOP
Maybe even admit I was wrong...
??
But I was too late.
THAT'S MY *FRIEND*... WHAT HAPPENED?
SORRY, MISTER.
FELL DOWN THE STAIRS... *BROKEN NECK*.

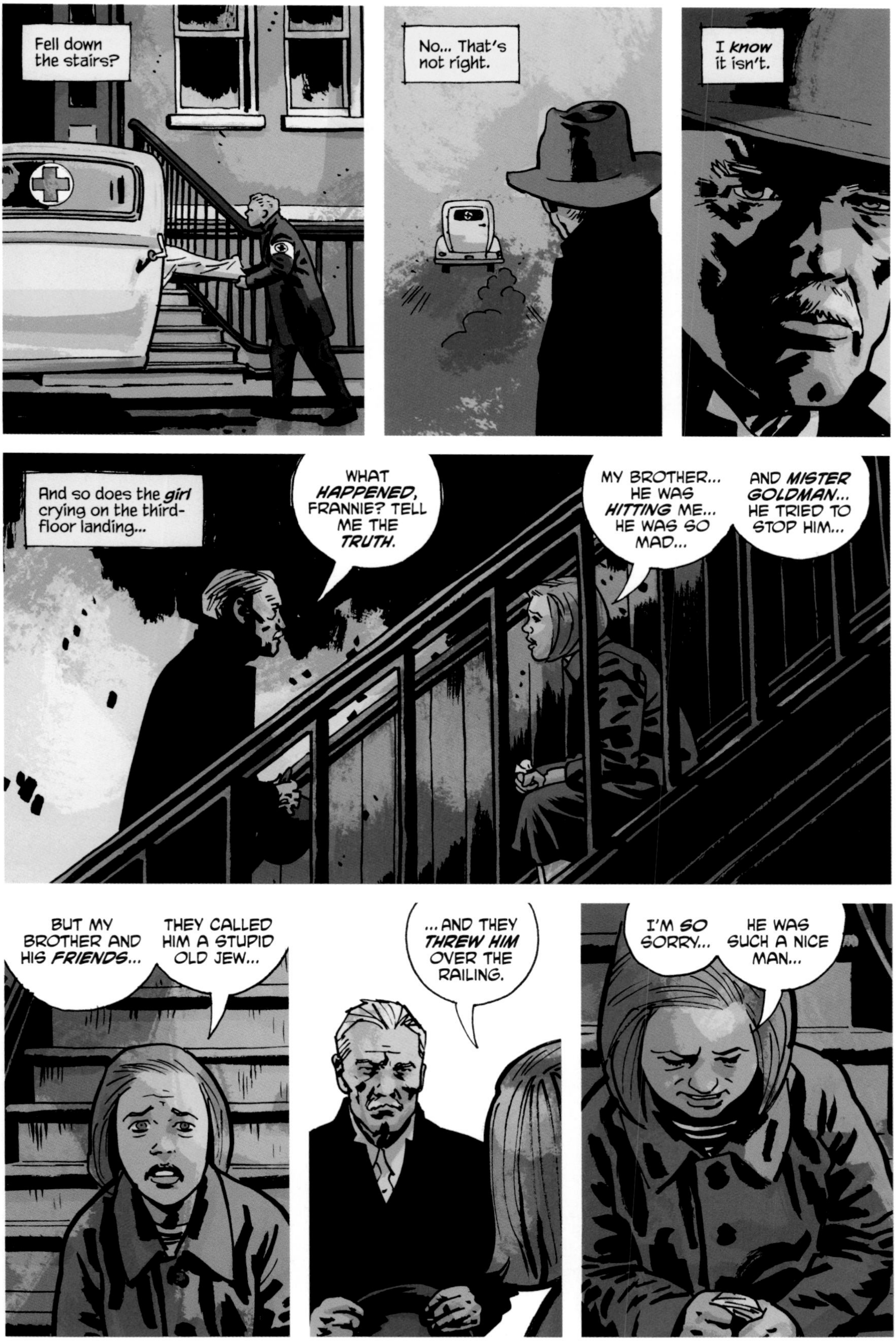
Fell down the stairs?
No... That's not right.
I *know* it isn't.
And so does the *girl* crying on the third-floor landing...
WHAT *HAPPENED*, FRANNIE? TELL ME THE *TRUTH*.
MY BROTHER... HE WAS *HITTING* ME... HE WAS SO MAD...
AND *MISTER GOLDMAN*... HE TRIED TO STOP HIM...
BUT MY BROTHER AND HIS *FRIENDS*...
THEY CALLED HIM A STUPID OLD JEW...
...AND THEY *THREW HIM* OVER THE RAILING.
I'M *SO* SORRY...
HE WAS SUCH A NICE MAN...

WHAT'S YOUR BROTHER'S *NAME?*

WHAT? NO.

YOU CAN'T TELL THE *POLICE*, HE'LL KILL ME.

I'M NOT GONNA TELL *ANYONE*, FRANNIE...

JUST GIVE ME HIS NAME.

In Jeremiah's apartment I find everything I need for what comes next.

My pistol from the night of the robbery...

His sawed-off shotgun...

And the *map* tacked up to his wall.

The other places where *Frannie's brother* and his friends can be found.

Yorkvale

Bohemia Beerhaus Bund-Only Club

The strange thing is, I don't even feel like I'm making a decision here.

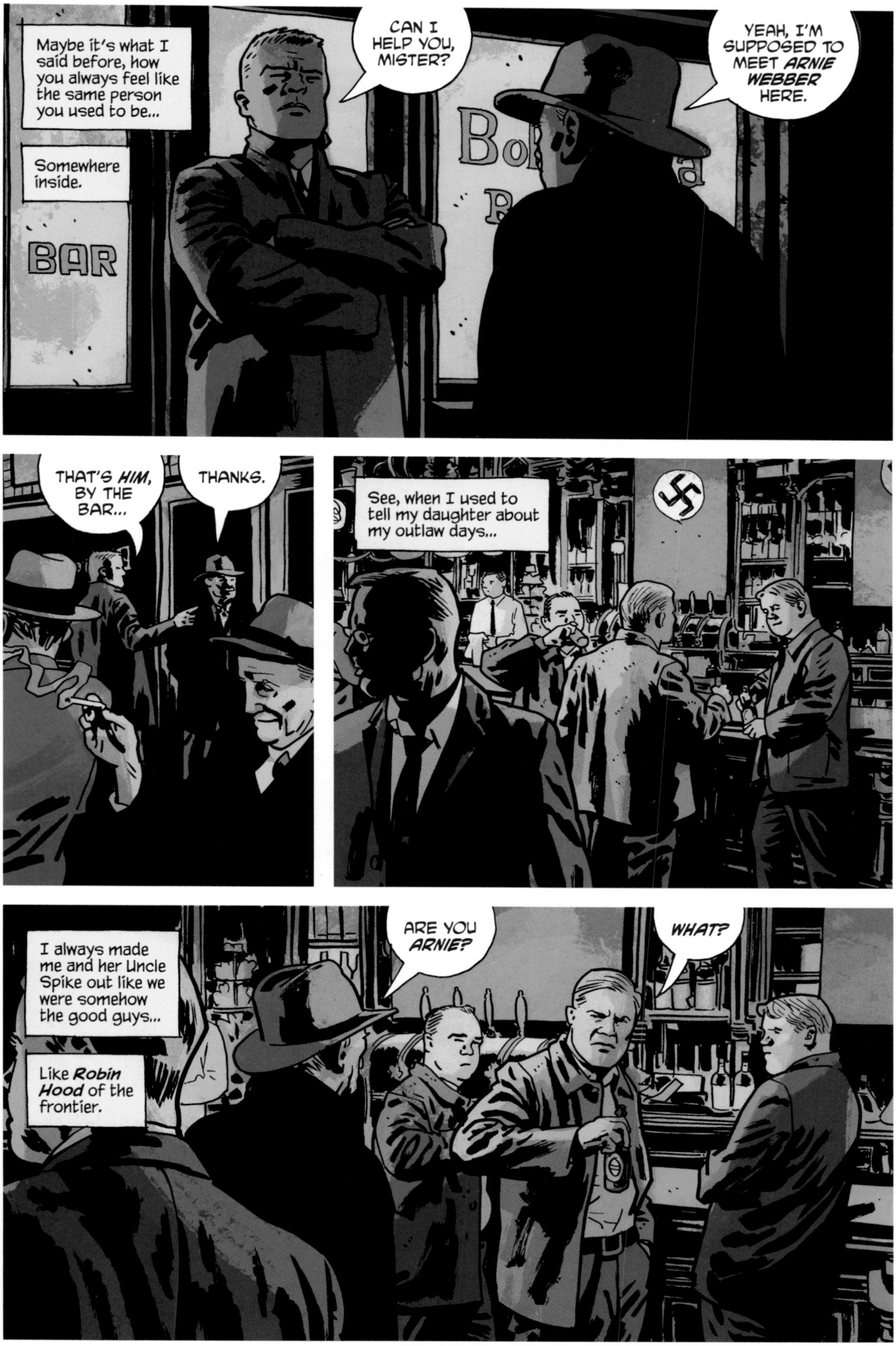
Maybe it's what I said before, how you always feel like the same person you used to be...
Somewhere inside.
BAR
CAN I HELP YOU, MISTER?
YEAH, I'M SUPPOSED TO MEET *ARNIE WEBBER* HERE.
THAT'S *HIM*, BY THE BAR...
THANKS.
See, when I used to tell my daughter about my outlaw days...
I always made me and her Uncle Spike out like we were somehow the good guys...
Like *Robin Hood* of the frontier.
ARE YOU *ARNIE?*
WHAT?

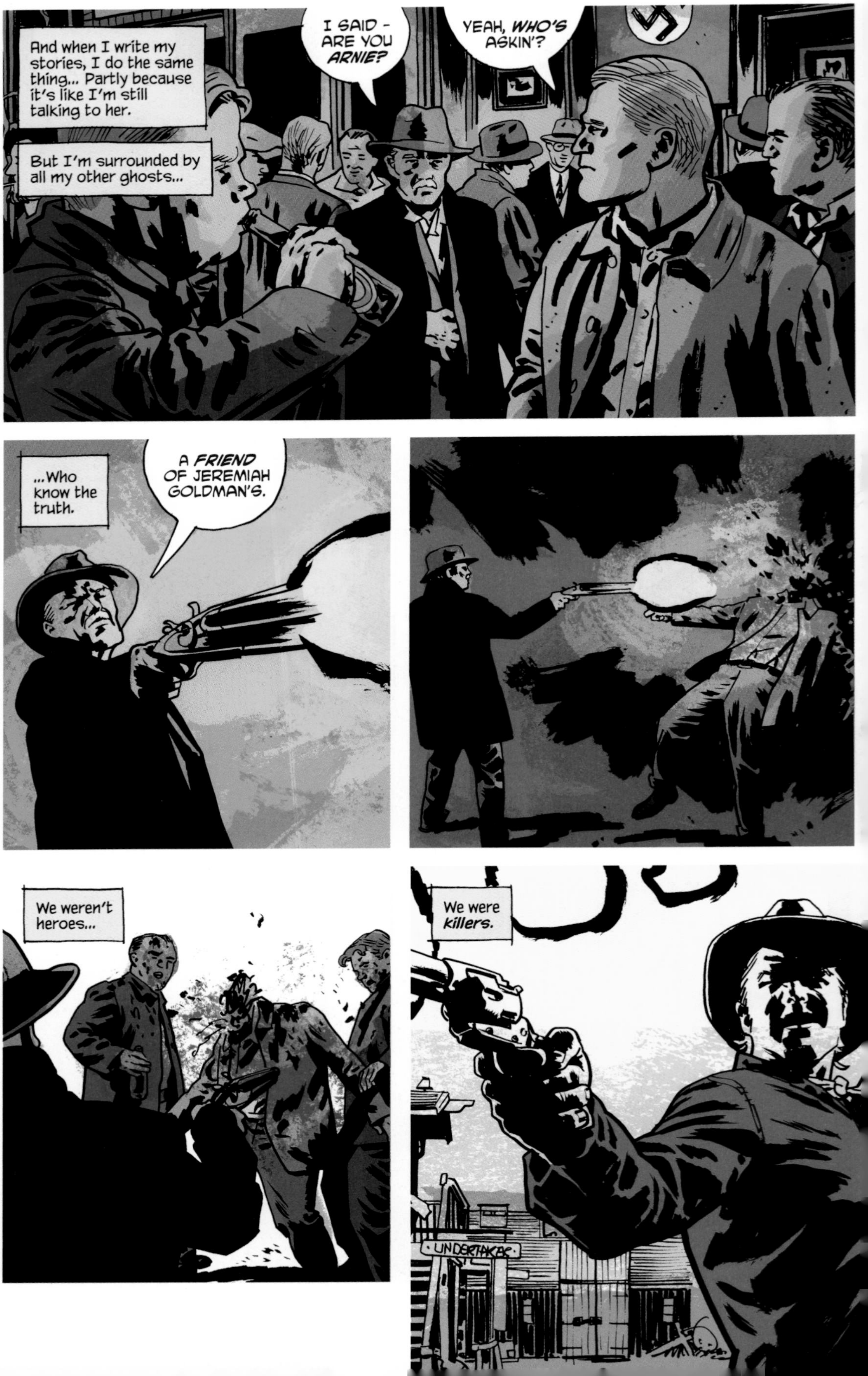
And when I write my stories, I do the same thing... Partly because it's like I'm still talking to her.
But I'm surrounded by all my other ghosts...
I SAID - ARE YOU ARNIE?
YEAH, WHO'S ASKIN'?
...Who know the truth.
A FRIEND OF JEREMIAH GOLDMAN'S.
We weren't heroes...
We were killers.
UNDERTAKER

That's the reason we survived so long...

Because this world belongs to the monsters.

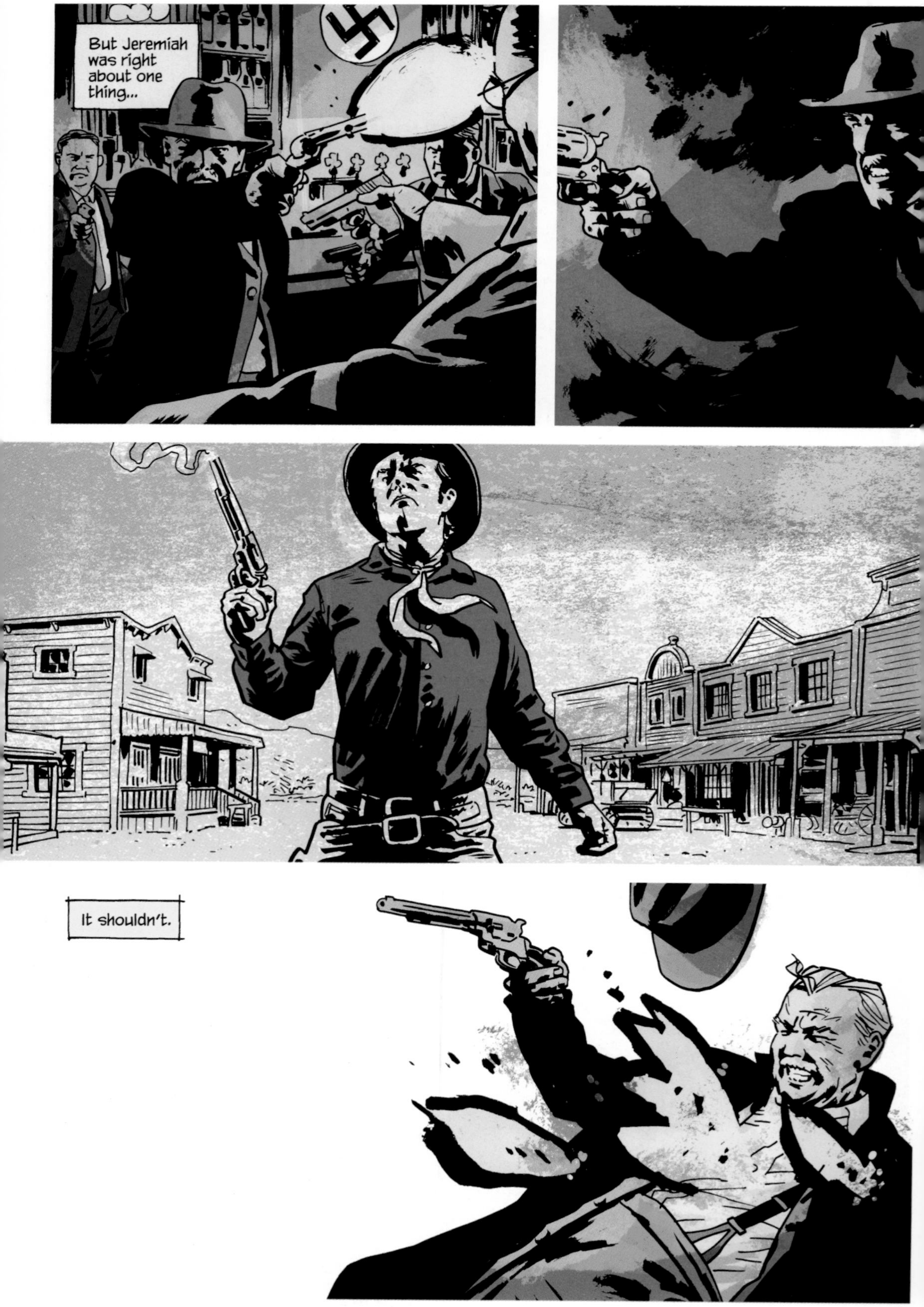
But Jeremiah was right about one thing...
It shouldn't.

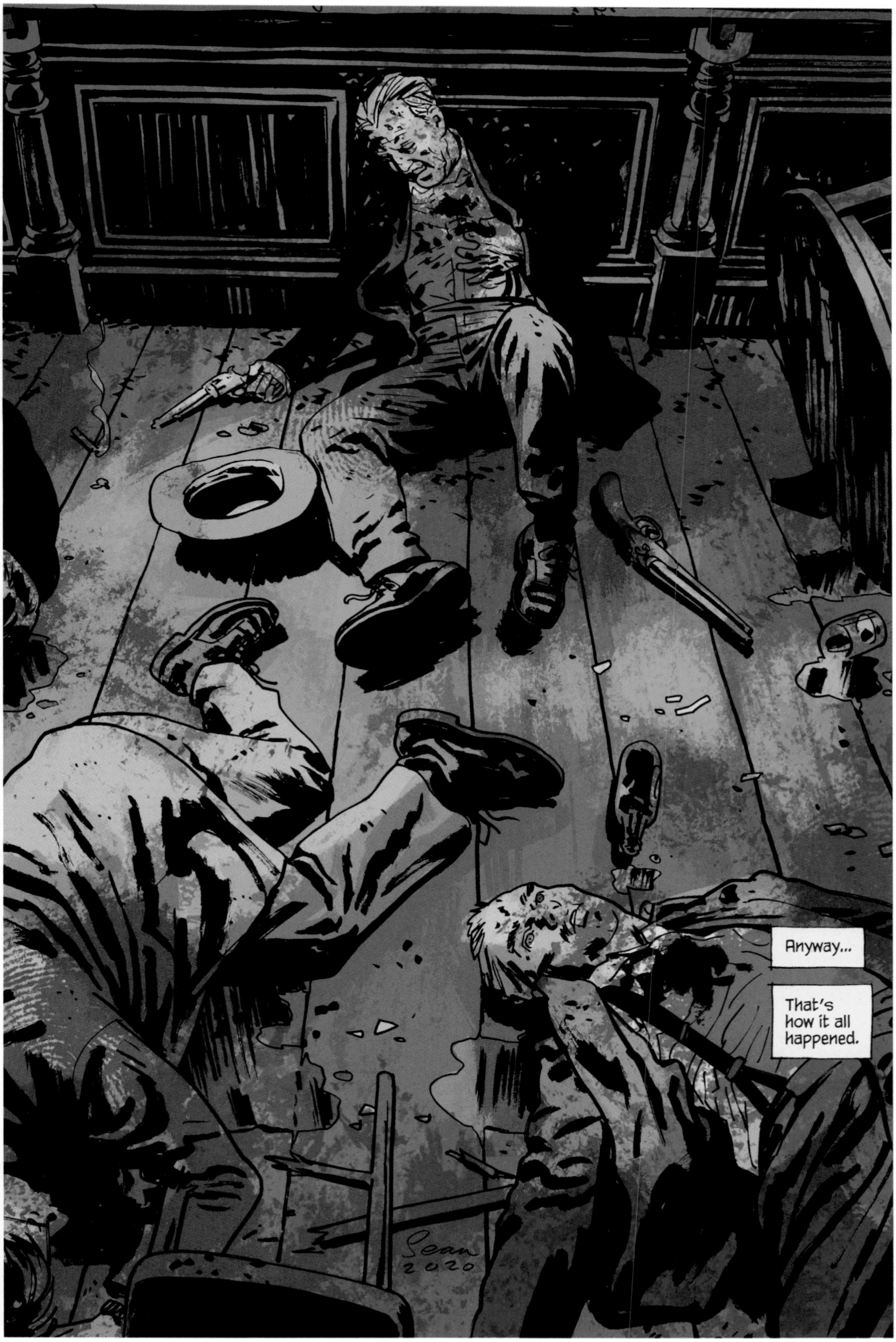
Anyway...
That's how it all happened.
Sean 2020

OTHER BOOKS BY BRUBAKER AND PHILLIPS:

CRIMINAL: Coward	ISBN: 978-1-63215-170-4
CRIMINAL: Lawless	ISBN: 978-1-63215-203-9
CRIMINAL: The Dead And The Dying	ISBN: 978-1-63215-233-6
CRIMINAL: Bad Night	ISBN: 978-1-63215-260-2
CRIMINAL: The Sinners	ISBN: 978-1-63215-298-5
CRIMINAL: The Last Of The Innocent	ISBN: 978-1-63215-299-2
CRIMINAL: Wrong Time, Wrong Place	ISBN: 978-1-63215-877-2
CRIMINAL The Deluxe Edition Volume One	ISBN: 978-1-5343-0541-0
CRIMINAL The Deluxe Edition Volume Two	ISBN: 978-1-5343-0543-4
FATALE Book One: Death Chases Me	ISBN: 978-1-60706-563-0
FATALE Book Two: The Devil's Business	ISBN: 978-1-60706-618-7
FATALE Book Three: West Of Hell	ISBN: 978-1-60706-743-6
FATALE Book Four: Pray For Rain	ISBN: 978-1-60706-835-8
FATALE Book Five: Curse The Demon	ISBN: 978-1-63215-007-3
FATALE The Deluxe Edition Volume One	ISBN: 978-1-60706-942-3
FATALE The Deluxe Edition Volume Two	ISBN: 978-1-63215-503-0
THE FADE OUT	ISBN: 978-1-5343-0860-2
THE FADE OUT Deluxe Edition	ISBN: 978-1-63215-911-3
KILL OR BE KILLED Volume One	ISBN: 978-1-5343-0028-6
KILL OR BE KILLED Volume Two	ISBN: 978-1-5343-0228-0
KILL OR BE KILLED Volume Three	ISBN: 978-1-5343-0471-0
KILL OR BE KILLED Volume Four	ISBN: 978-1-5343-0651-6
KILL OR BE KILLED The Deluxe Edition	ISBN: 978-1-5343-1360-6
BAD WEEKEND	ISBN: 978-1-5343-1440-5
MY HEROES HAVE ALWAYS BEEN JUNKIES	ISBN: 978-1-5343-1515-0
CRUEL SUMMER	ISBN: 978-1-5343-1643-0